Amigas
Fifteen Candles

Amigas
Fifteen Candles

by Veronica Chambers

Created by Jane Startz
Inspired by Jennifer Lopez

SCHOLASTIC INC.
New York Toronto London Auckland
Sydney Mexico City New Delhi Hong Kong

ISBN 978-0-545-29350-1

12 11 10 9 8 7 6 5 4 3 2 1   10 11 12 13 14 15/0

Printed in the U.S.A.   40

First Scholastic printing, September 2010

Designed by Jennifer Jackman

Por mi Flora
—V.C.

To my amazing family: Peter, Jesse, Kate, and Zoë
—J.S.

CHAPTER 1

ALICIA CRUZ had the good fortune of being born into wealth, but not spoiled by it. She was pretty but real, which meant boys liked her and girls wanted to be her friend. She had *caramelo* skin, big brown eyes, and wavy brown hair. Most of all, she was kind and creative—which together made for a very winning combination.

For as long as anybody could remember, whenever there was any kind of show involving dancing, Alicia was the force behind it. In second grade, Alicia recruited her friend Carmen to star in her rendition of *You're a Good Man, Charlie Brown*. Carmen was a Glamazon: six feet tall by the ninth grade and racially ambiguous.

Italians thought she was Italian. French people thought she was French. Japanese people thought she was part Japanese. Whenever Alicia and her crew hung out in South Beach, tourists would always stop Carmen and ask her directions in various languages. Carmen Ramirez-Ruben *was* mixed: her mother was Mexican American and her father was Jewish and Argentinean. But Carmen said that that was what made living in Miami so cool—almost everybody was from somewhere else. Although Carmen could totally have been a model, her passion was designing clothes.

In the sixth grade, determined to be the next Gwen Stefani, Alicia introduced herself to the cute new boy, Gaz (short for Gaspar) Colón, and recruited him to join her short-lived ska band. Gaz was from Puerto Rico and had moved to Miami at the end of elementary school. He was the only one in their crew who was completely fluent in Spanish; everybody else spoke varying degrees of Spanglish. Gaz could not only roll his *R*'s like a pro, he had an amazing singing voice. His dad, who had died when Gaz was just a kid, had been a big-time singer in San Juan. Now his mother worked as a cleaning woman for a really rich Panamanian family in the Gables. Gaz always said he and Alicia were *como herma-nos*. Which was why Alicia was trying very hard not to think about how good-looking Gaz had become since they had started high school: how weird would it be to be totally hot for your adoptive big brother?

Alicia met Jamie Sosa in the eighth grade, when she started taking break-dancing classes and heard there was a new girl from the Bronx who bought and sold the coolest Japanese sneakers online. Jamie's family was from the D.R., but until she moved to South Beach in the eighth grade, she had lived in New York.

Jamie was the queen of hip-hop chic. She was beyond cool, she was cutting-edge. If Jamie got a haircut, the next thing you knew, it would be in *People*, rocked by all the hottest stars. If Jamie rocked wide-legged pinstriped pants, then three months later, there'd be a whole story on that *exact* pair of pants in *InStyle* magazine. Sometimes Alicia thought that Jamie had ESP—or that she was the style equivalent of James Bond: a secret-agent fashionista who spent her weekends jetting around to L.A., New York, and London, picking up on all of the latest trends.

By ninth grade, they were a posse—Alicia, Jamie, Gaz, and Carmen. They weren't the most popular kids at Coral Gables High—lemmings are lemmings, even in a place as fabulous as South Beach. At Alicia's school, as at almost every other place in the Western world, the football players and the cheerleaders ruled. But Alicia and her friends were fairly confident that, of all the groups and social sectors that dominated the school—including the jocks and their babes, the socialist Che wannabes, and the Clockwork Cholas (the Latina Goths)—they had the most fun.

Fun was, after all, in Alicia's DNA. Every year, her parents held a Winter Wonderland party and covered their massive front lawn with fake snow. Over a hundred people showed up to make snowballs and snowmen and, of course, snow angels. Maribelle Puentes, the Cruzes' cook and house-keeper, who had worked for the family since Alicia was a baby, passed out *copitas* of hot chocolate and made s'mores in the outdoor fireplace.

In the summer, the Cruzes' Memorial Day weekend pool party was the most coveted invitation in town. The party started promptly at six p.m. with a massive *barbacoa* and ended with a huge pancake breakfast in the pool house at six in the morning. Alicia's mom was a judge, and her father was the deputy mayor. Everybody knew they had a strict no-alcohol rule at their parties, so all the parents at C. G. High were cool with their kids' going to the Cruzes' fiestas. All in all, life was pretty sweet for the four friends, and they didn't have much to complain about—usually. . . .

Saturday night found Jamie, Carmen, Alicia, and Gaz at a very undesirable, very noisy, and very dimly lit table next to the kitchen all the way in back of the grand ballroom of the Coronado hotel in downtown South Beach. Alicia's parents were seated near the front, at a table with a group of promi-nent *padres*, including the governor and his wife. A ballroom full of teenagers socializing while dressed in promworthy clothes with all of their parents, albeit at separate tables, could mean only one thing—*quinceañera* season had begun.

In the rest of the U.S., socially ambitious high school students competed to outshine the antics seen on *My Super Sweet 16*. But in Miami, it was all about the *super sweet 15s*, or *quinceañeras*, as the parties were officially known. In a tradition that dated back to the eighteen hundreds, *quinceañeras* were a coming-of-age ritual, for girls only, that was celebrated throughout Latin American culture. When you turned fifteen, or *quince años*, you become a woman in the eyes of your family, your friends, and the community. In a city where the word *Latino* referred to the heritage of dozens of countries, skin tones, and beliefs, the *quince* parties were a unifying force. Many parents started saving for a *quince* as soon as a baby girl was born, and just as many spent thousands upon thousands of dollars on their daughter's event. As big as a wedding, a *quinceañera* included all of your family, all of your parents' friends, and a "court" of seven girls and seven boys called *damas* and *chambelanes*. There was a traditional father-daughter dance called the *vals*, a church ceremony, a speech, bands, DJs, and tons of food. *My Big Fat Greek Wedding* had nothing on these big phat *quinces*.

Alicia and her *amigas* called it *quince* season, because even though girls had birthdays all year round, there were certain times of the year that were *quince* blackouts. No one wanted a *quince* that would have to compete with the festivities of Thanksgiving or Christmas. Spring was also not the best time for a *quince*—too many prom and graduation parties to steal your shine. The best time for a *quince* was right at the beginning of the summer, before people went away to camp or traveled with their family, and the second best time was in the fall, when school started back up again. At least, that's the way it was in Miami.

It was June now, and Simone Baldonado, whose family was loaded, had invited Alicia, her friends, and half of Miami–Dade County to the first big *quinceañera* of the summer. Alicia sighed. She knew that by the time January rolled around, she would have been to twenty parties, easy.

One of the unspoken rules of the *quince* was that no one ever brought dates—too much scrutiny from the 'rents and all their friends. The best strategy, one that Alicia and her friends had been employing for the last two years, since the girls they had grown up with started turning fifteen, was to:

1. dress cute, because being tagged, then trying to untag yourself and being tagged again on Facebook was part of the battle royal of *quinces*, and
2. roll as a crew, dance with whomever you wanted when you got there, but show up together. And leave together. No *quince* partygoer gets left behind.

Employing said strategy, Jamie was, at that moment, dancing to a Daddy Yankee song with Gabriel, who was— they had all agreed earlier in the ladies' room—M-W-A-H

(*Man, What a Hottie*), with extra sauce on the W-A-H. Carmen, the aspiring fashion designer, was camped out next to the dance floor, doing sketches of the best dresses at the party, which left Gaz and Alicia alone at their table. Alicia couldn't help it—she flushed—something she had been doing, despite her best intentions, a lot around Gaz lately.

But how could she not? Gaz looked superhandsome in his *quince* uniform: a cream-colored shirt with a charcoal gray pin-striped vest and matching pants. It was a uniform because, unless a guy was a *chambelán*, he really needed only one *quince* outfit a year. Girls, on the other hand, needed a whole wardrobe of party dresses. Or at least three. Alicia was wearing a turquoise blue one-shoulder Alice + Olivia dress. Sitting next to Gaz at a candlelit table covered in rose petals, Alicia could almost pretend that the other people at the party didn't exist. Even though she wouldn't admit it to the others, she had it bad for Gaz. But he was her friend. It *had* to stay that way—right?

"I like it back here," Gaz said, interrupting her thoughts. "It's like being in the back of the school bus."

"I guess," Alicia said, nodding. "But this is only the first *quince* of the season, and I'm already tired of it all."

"It's not so bad. *Quinces* are a good excuse to dress up, go out somewhere fancy, eat for free." Gaz's hand hovered just above hers.

Alicia thought about being brazen and just grabbing his hand and holding it. She had an intense urge to touch him. Where had it come from? And why now, when she'd known him all these years? Her emotions were driving her crazy! She shook her head, and then, instead of taking hold of his hand, she hit him with a platonic fist bump instead. She was such a chicken!

"What was that?" Gaz asked, his voice playful.

Alicia's cheeks grew red. Was he flirting with her? "I don't know," she said. "What do you think it was?"

"What's up, guys?" Jamie asked, as she plopped down at the table.

"Not much," Alicia said, trying not to groan. Talk about bad timing!

At that moment, the lights dimmed, and Carmen slid back into her seat.

"Okay, *amigas*," Carmen whispered. "The madness is starting."

On cue, Simone Baldonado walked onto the stage in a red dress with a gigantic train that looked as if it had been made from drapes from an old plantation, like that of Scarlett O'Hara's Tara in *Gone with the Wind*. It was only six p.m., but she was already on her third costume change of the day, having worn a scandalously short, sheer white minidress for the church ceremony and a black-and-white Marchesa gown to greet the guests as they arrived. Now she was wearing this red number.

Alicia had to admit that no matter what she wore, Simone always looked great. But as Gaz was fond of saying, "Pretty can't cover up crazy."

Simone walked up to the microphone and greeted the packed room. Simone's mom had told Alicia's mom that the grand ballroom seated a thousand, and every seat was taken—or so it seemed. "Good evening," Simone said. "As many of you know, my dream is to be an actress. So, for your viewing pleasure, my *damas*, my *chambelanes* and *moi* will not be performing any of the traditional *quince* dances. Instead we, I, will be performing a little piece I created called 'The Great Princesses of History.' Maestro—"

Simone signaled to the full orchestra, and they began playing a boisterous overture. She ran offstage, reappearing five minutes later in full Egyptian dress and some hastily applied kohl eyeliner.

"I am Cleopatra," she whispered into the microphone, before launching into a frenetic dance to the tune of "Walk Like an Egyptian."

When it was over, she ran offstage, changed, and came back out in a hoop-skirted ball gown and a white wig.

Approaching the microphone again, she said, "I am Marie Antoinette," then danced a positively mesmerizing number to Bow Wow Wow's "I Want Candy."

Once more she went offstage, then returned, this time in a futuristic white tunic and two doughnut buns on either side of her head; she declared, "I am Princess Leia." She solo-danced in this outfit to the Styx ("Mr. Roboto"), ending the dance by saying, "Help me, Obi-Wan Kenobi, you're my only hope."

Just when Alicia thought the performance couldn't go on any longer, a whole new part began. There were odes to the real Russian princess Anastasia and to Disney's Jasmine, and a very odd tribute to Prince's Princesses, in which Simone danced to a medley of "U Got the Look," "Diamonds and Pearls," and "Purple Rain."

Alicia and her friends, as well as most of the guests, were so shocked that they did not say anything for a very long time. But half an hour into Simone's show, Gaz broke the silence at their table.

"I'm bored out of my mind," he whispered.

"I'm stunned," Carmen said softly.

"I'm going with Gaz—'bored,'" yawned Jamie.

"I am, even if I hate to admit it, kind of impressed," Alicia said.

"Impressed?" Jamie said. "You're kidding, right? This is nothing more than the inner workings of a megalomaniac with a personality disorder."

"But, the sets, the costumes, the choreography!" Alicia insisted.

"It's all the self-indulgences of a spoiled rich girl," Jamie retorted. "I bet this little dance extravaganza costs more than my entire *quince*."

Jamie's *quinceañera* had been a house party, *and* the best one Alicia had ever attended. Jamie's cousin, Caterina, who was a DJ at Bungalow 8 in New York, had flown in and rocked the house, spinning hip-hop and reggaeton all night long. Jamie had looked amazing in a sleeveless Japanese T-shirt that Carmen had covered with hot pink sequins. She wore a long, hot pink ball-gown skirt that she'd found at a vintage shop and a pair of one-of-a-kind Bathing Ape boots that one of her eBay clients in Japan had sent her. Jamie had danced an amazing merengue for the *vals* with her dad, and her mother, who was an incredible cook, had made all of the food.

It had been everything a *quince* never was—fierce, fabulous, and flawless. But because it hadn't been in a hotel ballroom or a club, Jamie was always defensive about it. She acted as if everyone were always saying what a great *quince* it was because they felt sorry for her—which nobody ever did, because, though Jamie wasn't rich, she was the definition of cool.

Alicia thought maybe Jamie was right; maybe another

over-the-top *quince* was just a waste of cash. But she'd always felt there was something feminist and badass about *quinces*. Life as a Latina could often mean being treated like a girl— and not in a good way. If you had a brother, he got more of everything: more freedom, more attention, more cash. It was always: "A son! What a blessing!"; "Look at my son!"; "I'm going on a business trip, taking my son, showing him the ropes!"

But *quinceañeras* were strictly the *chicas'* terrain. If, every once in a while, a girl went *quince*-zilla and drove her friends and family crazy, then who could blame her? The *quince* was so much more than a party; it was a statement about the kind of girl you were and the kind of woman you hoped to become. You only got one shot, and *claro*, you wanted it to be perfect.

The lights had dimmed once again. Looking up at the stage, Alicia saw that Simone was now dressed in a floor-length baby blue evening gown. She was also sporting a blond wig.

"What—," Alicia began.

"The hell—," Jamie continued.

"Is she up to?" Carmen said, finishing the thought.

"My final number is a tribute to Princess Diana," Simone said. "England's rose. The people's princess."

"No, she didn't," Jamie whispered.

Alicia whispered back, "Oh, yes, she did."

"Does she know this is borderline offensive?" Carmen added.

Gaz laughed. "Do *you* know that Simone is the definition of 'borderline'?"

When the songs—and performance—were *finally* over, there was an uncomfortable silence, followed by tepid and confused applause. Simone seemed oblivious. "Okay, enough of that," she said. "Let's *salsa*!"

But Gaz was clapping wildly. Apparently he had had a change of heart. "I love it," he said. "She's a total nut job. Now, this is what I call living *la vida loca*."

Alicia lifted a glass of fruit punch and saluted her friends: "One crazy *quince* down, a kazillion more to go. Here's to summer!"

As she clinked her glass with the others', Alicia took in their smiling faces—Jamie's sideways diva smirk; Carmen's intense green eyes and wide grin; Gaz's *mwah*dom—and thought, I could not have picked a cooler bunch of friends if I had searched the whole entire world.

CHAPTER 2

ALICIA HAD been wanting a real summer job since junior high. Finally, after her freshman year, her father agreed that she was old enough to apply for internships. She'd applied at both City Hall and *Ocean Side* magazine. But she knew that she wanted to be at City Hall. She and her dad were tight, and secretly, she thought someday she'd like to run for office, too. Now that Sonia Sotomayor was a Supreme Court justice, Alicia thought the country might just be ready for a Latina president.

After some intense interviews—and a rather huffy rejection from *Ocean Side* (apparently they did not think a person with no journalistic experience was worth their time)—Alicia had landed the internship at City Hall. Even though she was supernervous at the additional work and a little bummed that her summer wasn't completely carefree, Alicia was excited.

Monday was the first day of her internship, and Alicia was dressed to impress. She'd put on a pale pink seersucker jacket, white pants, and her favorite beaded Alice + Olivia T-shirt. Her father had offered her a ride to the office, but Alicia wanted to make her own introductions, not just arrive as the daughter of the deputy mayor. So she'd taken the bus and arrived at 8:15 a.m., even though her letter said she wasn't due until nine.

The intern supervisor, Lori Evans, came in at 8:45, and Alicia jumped up to meet her, shaking her hand vigorously. Lori was a tall blond woman, dressed in a taupe linen suit that only served to highlight the fact that she was the palest human being in the Greater Miami area. She spoke in a flat South Florida drawl as she led Alicia back to her office, which Alicia was pretty sure had recently been a broom closet. Alicia had to wonder if it was the humble surroundings, or just her personality, that caused Lori to behave like the grinch that stole summer vacay.

"You know," Lori said, as Alicia sat, slightly tremulous, across from her, "I'm too busy to hold your hand, so pay attention. Coffee machine is over there. Copy machine is in the back room. Don't steal supplies, because I'm watching you. Don't come in late, because I'm watching you."

Alicia decided it wouldn't be wise to mention the time she'd gotten in. She'd dealt with this kind of attitude before. Sometimes, when people knew who her father was, they went out of their way to give her the rich-girl smack-down. She had learned to ignore it. Instead, she simply nodded and took careful notes on Lori's instructions.

"Don't try to kiss up by writing down every word I say," Lori growled. Her fingers fiddled with a cigarette that she seemed to be longing to smoke.

Alicia tried to keep from collapsing like a soufflé at the thought of spending the summer under the thumb of an angry-at-the-world human ashtray. She put her pen down.

"The copy machine requires a personalized code," Lori continued. "I track expenses, so don't think you can get away with making color copies of your favorite Jonas Brothers pictures." Lori paused to type something into her computer. She looked up at Alicia. "Your code is A51221."

Alicia nodded and tried to think of a system for remembering the code: *A*, her grade point average, if you didn't count physics; five, the number of inches tall her Mom's Fendi logo heels were; twelve, the number of Jesus's disciples; and twenty-one, the age she'd be when she graduated from college. Easy. Sort of.

"Aren't you going to write your code down?" Lori asked. "Do you think I have nothing better to do than to keep looking up a code you're going to need a hundred times a day?"

Alicia turned bright red. "But you said not to write everything down!"

Lori made a dismissive motion with her arm, as if Alicia were dumb as a board. "Go to your desk, Miss Cruz, and make yourself useful. Did I tell you where the coffee machine is?"

Alicia nodded. "Yes, but I don't drink coffee."

"Not for you, for me," said Lori. "I require a fresh cup of coffee with hazelnut creamer and four teaspoonsful of sugar every three hours. Don't make me ask twice—and don't leave the coffee to get cold if I'm out on a smoke break. Wait till I get back, got it?"

Alicia assured her that she had.

All that had been exactly seventy-six minutes ago, and apart from her father's calling to check on her ("Yes, *Papi*, I'm fine—just peachy. Lori? She's a hoot."), Alicia had done absolutely nothing at her fancy internship but make regular updates to her Facebook page.

Alicia Cruz Is excited to be starting an internship in the mayor's office of the best city in the world—Miami!
9:14 a.m. 🔒 · Comment · Like

Alicia Cruz Hopes that she gets to work on some fun projects.
9:28 a.m. 🔒 · Comment · Like

Alicia Cruz Doesn't drink coffee, but may need to start because the boredom is *deep*.
9:32 a.m. 🔒 · Comment · Like

Alicia Cruz Is wondering if anyone would notice if she slipped out for *un rato* to go to the beach.
10:52 a.m. 🔒 · Comment · Like

"The answer is yes. They'd notice."

Alicia jumped. She hadn't realized there was a girl standing behind her. She was petite, with straight brown hair. She was also curvy in all the right places—like Salma Hayek's mini-me. She was wearing a girlie pink blouse with ruffles and an orange bouclé skirt. It wasn't Alicia's style, but the girl was rocking it.

"You must be Alicia Cruz," the girl said confidently.

"That's me," Alicia said, reaching out to shake the out-stretched hand.

"I'm Sarita Lopez. I just moved to town from Atlanta, and, since my school got out earlier than almost everyone's, I started working here, two weeks ago."

Sarita took a seat at the next desk, and it was all Alicia could do not to jump for joy. Maybe there was hope for this internship after all.

"So, have you met Lori?" Sarita asked as she sorted through a huge stack of papers on her desk.

"Uh, yeah," Alicia said. "I've also been sitting here, staring at my computer screen, for nearly two hours now. I say hello to people, but nobody stops to talk or to give me something to do."

"Trust me, I know," Sarita said. "I spent my entire first week getting Lori coffee and hanging out on Facebook. The thing is, everyone here is too busy to deal with the interns, even the intern supervisor. You've got to just go to a department and tell them you'll do anything: get them lunch, make copies, do research at the library."

Alicia nodded. Sarita's advice made sense. "It would've been nice if my dad had given me a heads-up," she said. But then it hit her: her father had no clue what life was like as a lowly intern. He was one of the busy people.

"Does your dad work here?" Sarita asked.

Alicia nodded. "Yeah, but he's in a different department."

Of course, at that very moment, Lori walked by. "Her father is the deputy mayor," she said. "So don't let her try to get you to do all of her work."

It took every ounce of control for Alicia not to roll her eyes.

Lori walked away, and Alicia wondered if Sarita were now going to start giving her attitude. But Sarita just said, "Deputy mayor, nice." Then, turning toward Lori's closed office door, she added, "Don't hate the player, hate the game, honey."

Alicia grinned. Sarita was cool. "So, what are you working on?" she asked.

Sarita smiled and began stapling sheets of paper. "I talked my way into a hybrid-and-alternative-fuel project with the Miami Green department."

Alicia was impressed. "That sounds pretty sweet," she said.

"I'm a science geek, so it's perfect," Sarita said, shrugging.

Alicia flipped through the departmental guide to the

mayor's office. "I have no idea where to begin."

Sarita took a break from her stapling. "Well, what do you like to do?"

Alicia took a big breath. That was a complicated question. She decided to go with the simplest answer. "I've been taking dance classes since I was a kid, and I love to choreograph things for the annual school talent show. And I *love* pop culture. I was going to do an internship at *Ocean Side* magazine, but this was an opportunity too good to pass up. Oh, that, and *Ocean Side* denied me. But I figure this internship will help balance out all my dancing when it comes time to apply to college. I'm hoping for Harvard." Alicia smiled, suddenly sort of embarrassed. She'd just spilled—a lot. Luckily, Sarita seemed unfazed.

"Well, the Office of Film and Cultural Affairs is always looking for help," Sarita pointed out.

Alicia shot out of her chair, her eyes shining. "Oh, my God, I'm so there. Thank you."

"No problem," Sarita said, returning to the stacks of files on her desk. "You know, for an environmental department, Miami Green still generates a heck of a lot of paperwork."

An hour later, Alicia's desk was as crammed as Sarita's.

"What's all that?" Sarita asked.

"Film permits for people who want to film music videos in Miami." Alicia smiled.

"Anyone I would've heard of?"

"Hmmm, yeah," Alicia said. She began to rattle off a list of names: "Miley Cyrus, Lupe Fiasco, Franz Ferdinand, but even more, there are requests from groups I've never heard of, from all over the world—Japan, Brazil, Sweden, Jamaica, Bermuda."

"That's crazy; who knew Miami was so popular?" Sarita said.

"Not me," Alicia said. "I grew up here and, I love it, but I tend to take it for granted."

For the next few hours, Alicia and Sarita worked side by side in happy silence. Then Alicia realized that it was two in the afternoon and she hadn't had any lunch. "I'm starving!" she cried, glancing around the nearly empty office.

"Me, too," Sarita said. "Let's go up to the cafeteria. We can grab something and bring it back to our desks. Lori won't mind."

Just to be sure, before they went anywhere, Alicia made sure that Lori had a fresh cup of coffee, with hazelnut vanilla cream, and four sugars.

A few minutes later, they were back at their desks chowing down on City Hall burgers and Town Crier fries as they caught up on their personal e-mails. They both agreed that the Food Services attempt to give every item on the cafeteria menu a catchy name was a little corny.

Suddenly, Sarita let out a groan. Alicia looked up. "I've got a million things to do for my *quince*," Sarita said. "My mom e-mails me about it every hour on the hour. Since we're new, we don't even know where to start. My uncle lives here; he's one of the mayor's aides, that's how I got this internship. But he's single, and he doesn't have kids, so he knows *nada* about *quinces*."

Alicia smiled. This was something she could handle. "I could help you out if you needed it. I *am* something of a *quince* expert, you know."

Sarita looked impressed. "Expert, huh? Did you have multiple *quinces* or something? I heard that girls down here are serious about their *quinceañeras*."

"Actually, I took a trip abroad for my *quince*, but I've *been* to *hundreds* of them," Alicia said.

Sarita raised an eyebrow. "Wow. That is a lot of friends."

"Who said anything about friends?" Alicia cracked. "Maybe it's not hundreds, but believe me, I've been to a lot. So, when is your *quince*?"

"In a little over a month," Sarita said.

Alicia tried not to fall off her very unergonomic office chair. "You're kidding, right?"

"Nope. Five weeks from Saturday. My mom's already invited all of our relatives in Atlanta, and they've booked their tickets. We just need to find a place."

Alicia looked stricken. What had Sarita and her mother been thinking? There was planning to be done. Dresses to be bought. Dances to be learned. It would take months!

"Five weeks isn't enough time to plan a *quinceañera*," Alicia said, trying to sound calm.

"Sure it is," Sarita said. "We don't have a ton of money, and I'm not planning on anything fancy."

Alicia breathed a sigh of relief. If small was the plan, maybe Sarita could pull it off. She'd honestly been afraid that her sudden panic was going to cause some very unsightly sweat marks on her seersucker jacket (which, to be perfectly honest, was her mother's seersucker jacket that she'd *sort* of borrowed). "So you're having a house party?" she asked.

Sarita shook her head. "No can do. Me and my mom are in a tiny condo on the beach, and we're expecting more than seventy-five people."

Alicia pulled her dark hair up into a ponytail. It was time to get down to business. She liked Sarita, and moreover, she felt as though she could really help her.

She began with the basics. "Okay, you need a hall. So what's your theme?"

Sarita shrugged.

Then Alicia asked, "Well, what kind of dress are you going to wear?"

Sarita shrugged again.

"And your *quince* is only five weeks away?" Alicia said. "What are you thinking, *niña*?"

"I don't know. In Atlanta, none of my friends had a *quince*. That's why they're all excited to come down here for mine."

Alicia nodded, but she couldn't help thinking that Sarita's friends were going to be sorely disappointed in a *quince* that had been put together with spit and Scotch tape in five weeks' time.

She took a deep breath. She wouldn't let that happen. "Your *quince*'s going to be great," she said, her voice full of determination. "And I'm going to help you."

"Believe me, *chica*. I appreciate it," Sarita said, jumping up. "But right now it's time for Lori's afternoon coffee, and trust me, we don't want the natives to get restless!"

CHAPTER 3

LATER THAT night, on Facebook, Alicia researched *quinceañera* planning online. She was shocked to see that the My *Quince* Sux group had 15,000 friends! It was full of girls whose *quinces* had caused them more drama than the antics of Britney, Paris, and the Gossip Girls combined. There were also ads for girls who were desperately seeking help in planning their Sweet Fifteen parties. It turned out that Sarita was far from being the only *quince* in distress. In the Miami group's page, Alicia found a *lot* of cries for help.

Una Flaca Desesperada wrote

DESPERATELY SEEKING DJ AND DANCE CREW FOR SOUTH
BEACH SWEET 15!
I love cumbria, hip-hop and reggaeton *pero* my *familia* doesn't
have the Benjamins to get a big name group like the Barranquilla
Boyz or Luis Boom. Newbie talent that can rock to a Latin beat
would be fine with me. If you have any suggestions, please contact
me *lo más pronto que posible! Gracias!*

Lola wrote

Hey, my *quince* is on November 10 and I have no clue how to do it. Can anyone recommend a step-by-step guide to hooking up a cool *quinceañera*? Please, I'm begging you! My mom has no idea either, 'cause she didn't do it for my sister and now I'm getting a double dose of her tacky ideas. What kind of other themes can I do besides the played out (and super childish) Cinderella? Sooooo boring and I hate pumpkins. Please help me ASAP.

Sylvia wrote

Hey, I'm in trouble. My family thinks a Sweet 15 dress has gotta be pink! I HATE PINK except as a hair color. All the padrinos and padrinas are probably going to be dressed in pink too. The decorations, which my mama has already bought, are pink, and the cake she ordered is pink too. What do I do? Does anyone have any idea on how to save me from this cotton candy nightmare *quince*? THANK YOU IN ADVANCE!!!!

La Recesionista Fashionista wrote

OK. Where to start? Here's my problem. I will be having my *quince años* in March. I already have chosen the color theme and dresses—ivory for the *damas*, with azure scarves hanging down the back, and for the *chambelanes*—ivory suits with azure hankies in the pocket and azure feathers in their fedora hats. Yes, people, the clothes at my *quince* will be banging! But aside from the outfits, I'm completely lost. My parents are divorced and I live with my mom. She's not Latin like my *papi* and until I brought it up, she'd never even heard of a *quinceañera* before (*¡fíjense, chicas!*). Me and my *mamacita* need MAJOR help with EVERYTHING! (Except for the clothes, which, as I've mentioned, are bangin'!)

Alicia stayed up until two in the morning reading the message boards. By the time she went to sleep, she knew what she had to do. She was going to do *more* than just help Sarita pick a space for her *quince*. She and her girls, along with Gaz—and her brother Alex, if she could convince him—were going to take *quinceañeras* in Miami to a whole new level. She was going to start Amigas Incorporated, and it was going to be the hottest party-planning business in town.

The next morning, Alicia found Maribelle in the kitchen, making breakfast.

"*Buenos días*, Maribelle," Alicia said, giving her a kiss on the cheek. The older woman was like a grandmother to her, especially since both of Alicia's *abuelas* had passed away before she was born.

Maribelle handed her a plate. "Banana pancakes, but I made yours special, with strawberries," she said, in her warm, gently accented voice. "It's a beautiful day. You eat outside with your parents."

"*Gracias*," Alicia said, taking the pancakes and OJ that Maribelle handed her.

"You're welcome," Maribelle said.

"You're the best." Alicia planted a *besito* on Maribelle's cheek.

Maribelle put one hand on her hip and gave Alicia a saucy

look. "And you think I need you to tell me that? *Vaya.*"

Her parents were having breakfast by the pool. When she joined them, Enrique Cruz was reading the *Miami Herald*, and Alicia's mom, Marisol, was reading the *National Law Journal.* They both put down their papers when they saw their daughter.

"So, ready for your second day at City Hall?" Enrique asked.

"I'm loving it, *Papi,*" Alicia said. "The Office of Film and Cultural Affairs said they have enough paperwork to keep me busy all summer long, and I really like the other high school intern. As a matter of fact, I'm helping her with a special project."

"Oh, really?" Mrs. Cruz said, raising an eyebrow. "What's that?"

"I'm helping her plan her *quince,*" Alicia said, nabbing a piece of her mom's toast. "I'm thinking if it's a hit, then me and my friends could even make it a business—a *quinceañera*-planning business."

Her parents exchanged glances. Alicia knew why. This wasn't the first business that she had started and, in short order, abandoned. In sixth grade, she had started a dog-walking service and worked her way up to walking five dogs every day, after school. Two weeks later, she'd quit, once it had become clear that the logistical nightmare of walking five dogs at once was nothing compared to the smell bomb of cleaning up five dogs' poop.

In eighth grade, Alicia and Carmen had started a baby-sitting business. But two weeks and twenty-four explosive diapers later, they'd come to the same conclusion—baby-sitting, like dog walking, involved a whole lot of poop for not a lot of cash.

Last summer they'd spent some time working on a vintage scarf business; they were going to sell the scarves, with Jamie's help, on eBay. But after a month of scouring all of Miami's best vintage shops and finding a really cool lamp for Alicia's room and a great dressmaker's dummy for Carmen's designs, they'd decided not to go into the vintage scarf business after all.

But all that was in the past. Alicia was convinced that the idea of a *quince*-planning business was, hands down, the best business plan that she had ever had.

Her mother smiled gently. "You know, you have a tendency to take on a lot, Lici," she said. "This internship in the mayor's office will look *so* good on your college application. I would hate to see anything jeopardize it."

"You know what *quinces* are like in Miami," Alicia said. "If my business is so successful that I have to give up my internship to run it, then I've got to do what I've got to do."

Alicia's mom rolled her eyes. It was just like Alicia to go

from zero to sixty when dreaming up new ideas. "Oh, yes, because every Ivy League college in the country is going to turn down a mayoral intern in favor of a girl who runs a party-planning business. Those party-planners always make dean's list and are an asset to every intellectual community."

Alicia couldn't believe what her mother was saying. She had *always* been an A student, except for math, and her mom knew just how hard Alicia had worked to eke out a B in honors calculus. But her mom was clearly in rare form today, and when Mrs. Cruz was like that, arguing with her was nothing more than a colossal waste of time. "You will give one hundred and ten percent to this internship and you will thank your lucky stars that your father was able to create such a wonderful opportunity for you at the eleventh hour," Mrs. Cruz added. "Help your friend out if you must, but you will not waste your entire summer planning parties."

"A *quinceañera* is more than a party, *Mami*," Alicia said. "It's a sacred ritual. It's a way to connect to our community and our heritage."

Her mom considered this, and when she spoke, her voice was slightly less severe. "It's a sacred ritual for *some* people," she said matter-of-factly. "It's a way for *some* people to connect to their community and to their heritage."

Alicia knew that her mother was referring to the class differences that were demonstrated with respect to *quinces*.

Among her parents' friends, most of the girls—following their parents' desire to be more American—didn't have *quinceañeras*. They had Sweet Sixteen parties, or their parents offered them a trip—to Buenos Aires or Madrid or Punta Cana—for their fifteenth birthday instead. *Quinces* were most popular among Latinas who lived in Latino neighborhoods and retained closer ties to their *patria* than Alicia's parents did. When Alicia had turned fifteen, six months before, she had taken the trip her parents offered her and spent ten days in Barcelona, with a side trip to Bilbao.

"Just because your friends don't have *quinces* for their daughters doesn't mean it's not an important part of *nuestra cultura*," Alicia said.

Alicia's mom sighed loudly. "I think you are just trying to make me angry."

"*Quinces* are important, Mom!" Alicia cried.

"Alicia, watch your tone," her father said gently.

"No, they're impractical, and they're old-fashioned," Alicia's mother retorted. "Why are these parents spending all of this money on a party, when they could be using that money for college tuition? You didn't even want a *quince*. Now you want to spend your summer planning other people's *quinceañeras*? *Es una locura!*"

"Marisol, this is not a decision you are making as a judge on a bench," Mr. Cruz said. "I, for one, think it's great that Alicia is honoring her culture."

"I would much prefer it if Alicia would honor her culture with something more substantive than big-budget parties that put working-class people more into debt." And on that note, Marisol got up and walked into the house, slamming the door behind her.

Alicia looked at her father.

"Give her time," Mr. Cruz said. "She'll come around." He stood up, gave Alicia a squeeze on the shoulder, and followed his wife inside.

Sitting alone, Alicia wanted to cry. It was as though she and her mother were fighting about something much bigger than whether she was going to start a *quince* business. Her mother was wrong. She could do both jobs, and *both* were important.

That night, she didn't see her parents at dinner, as they had season tickets to the Miami Ballet. And the next morning, Alicia woke to find her father having breakfast alone.

"Good morning. Where's *Mami*?" she asked, kissing her father on the forehead. She loved his dark, curly hair with its silky threads of gray.

"She's already left for work," her father said, putting down his newspaper.

"I get it. She's mad at me, so she went in early," Alicia said, helping herself to the *fritura* that was on the table. Maribelle had outdone herself, and the Mexican ceramic serving plate was piled high with all of Alicia's favorite breakfast treats: empanadas, *carimonolas, croquetas.*

"Believe it or not, Alicia," her father said in a teasing tone, "the world doesn't revolve around you. Your mother had a lot of paperwork to catch up on at her office."

"Maybe so, but she's also furious at me," Alicia said. "It's not my fault if she wants to be a *gringa* American and I want to form a business to help my Latina sisters."

Enrique Cruz raised an eyebrow. "So that's what your business is about? Your Latina sisters?"

"Sorta," Alicia mumbled, her mouth full of food.

"I see," Enrique said.

"That's what *Mami* doesn't understand," Alicia went on. "If she knew anything about *quinces*, she wouldn't stand in the way of my business."

Alicia's father looked at his only daughter and wondered if she had any idea how much she and her mother were alike. Then he did what he did best: he played peacekeeper.

"Alicia, do you know that when your mother was your age, she wanted nothing more in the world than to have a *quinceañera* party?" Enrique asked.

"No," Alicia said with a sigh. She knew that tone of voice. It meant her father was going to tell her one of those stories about their immigrant background that would make her feel totally bad for her mom—and guilty for behaving, ever so slightly, like a spoiled brat.

"Well, she did," Enrique said. "You *do* know that your grandfather, Señor Toto, owned a shoe shop on Palmera Avenue?"

Alicia nodded. "The shoe repair shop."

Enrique shook his head. "That's the thing. Your grandfather did much more than repair shoes. He made custom shoes for the Miami Opera, for the mayor, and he did a brisk business in *quinceañera* heels. You've been to enough *quinces* to know the significance of the shoes in the *quince* ceremony."

Of course Alicia knew. The ceremony of changing from flats into high heels signified a girl's walk into womanhood. But her grandfather making *quinceañera* heels? And shoes for the opera? Her father had to be making this up.

"If *Abuelo* Toto was such a hotshot shoemaker, then how come he wasn't rich? And how come *Mami* couldn't have a *quince* if she wanted one?" Alicia asked.

"*Niña*," Enrique said, reaching out to squeeze his daughter's shoulder, "your grandfather was not Bill Gates. Making shoes is not like making computers. A custom-made shoe takes a very long time to create. The profit margin is very small. He did make a good living, but he poured it all into the education of his children. It takes a lot to send five kids to Catholic school and then to college, especially when your eldest daughter has got her heart set on a school like Harvard."

Alicia put her hands up in a gesture of mock surrender. "Okay, you win. I am officially a horrible, ungrateful American daughter and I will happily focus all my energy on my *unpaid* internship at City Hall. I mean, who wants to own her own business? Who wants to make money? Not me. That sounds awful. I will do my penance as a good Latina daughter."

Her father feigned surprise; his mischievous smile reminded Alicia of Antonio Banderas in the old Zorro movies.

"Did I make you feel guilty?" he asked sweetly. "That wasn't my intention."

He stood up from the breakfast table and picked up his paper and his book, a biography of Thomas Jefferson. Her father *loved* biographies.

"Don't give up on your idea yet, Lici," he said. "In the art of negotiation, there are always three ways of looking at an argument: your way, my way, and the third way."

"What does that even mean?" Alicia asked.

"The third way is the way of compromise," her father said, as he headed toward the garage.

Alicia stifled a groan. She hated word games. But one thing was for sure—no matter what she'd just told her dad, she would find a way to make Amigas Inc. work . . . *and* get her parents' approval. It might just take some time.

But before she could prove herself right, she had to actually *start* the business. To make that happen, she needed her peeps.

CHAPTER 4

THAT DAY at work, Alicia called her friends and asked if they wanted to come over for lunch on Saturday. She quickly explained about Sarita, then said they'd talk more when they met. It was not a hard sell. All of them liked to hang out at Casa Cruz, and not just because Alicia had a pool and Jacuzzi. The Key West–style house on Espanola Drive was beautiful without being flashy, like the other opulent homes in the neighborhood. There were two coral stone fireplaces, so during hurricane season, when it rained every other day, Alicia and her friends hung out in front of them, playing board games and chilling out. There was an exercise room with a huge flat-screen TV, a treadmill, an elliptical machine, free weights, and a Wii Fit. There was, of course, the pool. But the real reason that Alicia's house was the number one hangout was Maribelle.

Maribelle always kept the fridge fully stocked, and she seemed to delight in feeding Alicia and her friends. Eating at Alicia's was like going to a restaurant. All you had to do was go into the kitchen, give Maribelle a hug, and tell her what you wanted. Pizza with barbecue chicken? Coming right up. Puerto Rican *pasteles* with pork, or pressed Cuban sandwiches with ham and cheese? *Claro que sí.* Vanilla ice cream with homemade dulce de leche? *No problema.*

Even though she still felt guilty that her mom wasn't 100 percent behind it—she *had* said she could try if it didn't take away from the internship—Alicia couldn't wait to tell her friends about the Amigas plan. There were lots of *quince* services in Miami—caterers, photographers, dress shops, and party-planners—but Alicia felt as if their business would have an edge. The message boards on Facebook made one thing perfectly clear: most adults had no idea what girls really wanted. Alicia knew that she, Carmen, Jamie, and Gaz could do what old-school *quince* pros couldn't: something new, something fresh, and something fabulous.

By noon on Saturday, when Carmen, Jamie, and Gaz arrived, Alicia was bursting at the seams. They'd barely walked through the door and gathered in the Florida room, the bright indoor patio that overlooked the pool, when Alicia passed out the business plan she'd spent all week working on.

"So, I take it you've come up with an idea for where that girl Sarita can have her *quince*?" Jamie said. Alicia hadn't given them very many details.

"Even better," Alicia said, handing out the packets she'd photocopied at the office, using the code that Lori had warned her not to use for personal jobs.

"Wow, you really put some time into this, Lici," Carmen said, looking over the stapled packet.

"Well," Alicia said, "I was online the other night until two o'clock in the morning. There are hundreds—scratch that—thousands of girls just like Sarita, who want to have a fabulous *quince* and don't know how to do it. They need help with everything from negotiating with hopeless moms and pushy *tias* to picking out their dress, their music, and their theme. We are going to help them. *We're* starting a *quince* business!"

Gaz smiled, causing Alicia's heart to thump. He looked as if the idea were something he actually could get into. "This could be a great chance for my band to pick up some more gigs." He and his brothers had a Latin rock band called La Dulcinea, but it hadn't gone anywhere so far. It was more than a little tough to break into the Miami music scene, since the clubs were constantly booked with the biggest bands from Spain and Latin America.

"You have me down as the designer of all the *quince* dresses," Carmen said, looking at her packet. "I can't believe I never thought of that before! Those dresses cost a fortune in the stores. Even if I offer a supersteep discounted rate, I could still rake in the bucks."

"What about me?" Jamie asked. "Where do I fit in?" She

was wearing a red, yellow, and green tie-dyed T-shirt, a long denim skirt, and a Rasta cap. Alicia couldn't help thinking that only Jamie could pull off an outfit like that. If Alicia had worn a skirt below her knees, she'd have looked like a crazy grandmother.

"Image consultant, what else?" Alicia replied. "You're in charge of everything from hair and makeup to invitations and thank-you notes."

In addition to putting together the most stylish outfits, Jamie was a whiz with Photoshop. She made everything from cool birthday and Christmas cards to photo collages that she would then have printed on canvas.

"Your brother could do the sets or any decorations," Gaz offered.

"*That* is a genius idea," Alicia said. "I hadn't even thought of that. I mean, I thought we might need his help. Alex is taking a summer engineering course at the University of Miami, but that's only three days a week."

They were all so excited about the idea that they didn't notice that Maribelle was standing at the doorway.

"Knock-knock," she said. "Anybody hungry?"

"Oh, yeah!" Gaz called out. "What's for lunch?"

Maribelle put down a humongous tray. "Let's see, I've got ceviche, *tostones*, guacamole, tortilla chips, and I'll be right back with a pitcher of pomegranate punch."

"You are like a goddess to me," Alicia said, digging in.

"Me, too," Jamie added, reaching for the ceviche.

"Me, three," Carmen said, going for the guac.

Gaz stood up and walked over to Maribelle, who was so petite her head barely came up to his shoulders.

"*Eres un ángel*, Maribelle," Gaz said. "*Cásate conmigo y nos vamos a mi isla a vivir felizmente para siempre.*"

"Stop showing off with the Spanish," Alicia said. "I didn't get all of it, but I know that Maribelle does not want to marry you."

Maribelle just giggled and hit Gaz on the shoulder. "*Eres malo.*"

For a few minutes, there was nothing but the sound of contented chewing and plates being passed back and forth as everyone devoured the feast that Maribelle had prepared. Alicia broke the silence. "There is *one* little problem with my plan, guys."

"What's that?" Carmen asked, her long legs stretched so far under the coffee table that her electric blue toenails could be seen sparkling all the way on the other side.

"My mom and dad are worrying that the *quince*-planning will interfere with my internship," Alicia said. "They want me to focus on what will look good on my college applications."

"Won't starting your own megasuccessful party-planning

business look good on your college application?" Jamie asked.

"My point to them exactly," Alicia said.

"So, talk some more," Carmen said. "Your folks aren't unreasonable."

"Wish I could stay and help with the 'rent situation, but I've got to head out," Gaz said, suddenly standing up. "My shift at the Gap starts in an hour. But count me in."

"And, as you know, he's our ride," Jamie said, giving Alicia a hug. "But I'm in, too."

"I love this idea," Carmen said, trading high fives with Alicia. "I have to say one thing about you, Alicia Cruz, you know how to keep things interesting."

Alicia shrugged. "No matter what happens with my parents and the business, we've got to help Sarita out. I told her we would. So, can everybody meet tomorrow at eleven a.m.?"

Everybody could, and Alicia walked them out to Gaz's car, which was a rusty Toyota Corolla.

"Yo, Gaz, you need some new wheels. This car is seriously clashing with my outfit," Jamie said as she climbed into the front seat.

"Yeah, like you could wear those ridiculously high heels on the subway in New York," Gaz said.

"Yeah, whatever. You've never even been to New York," Jamie said.

Alicia and Carmen exchanged looks. Jamie and Gaz were always going at it. Maybe it was because they were so different: Jamie was this hard-core girl from the Bronx; Gaz was the sweet island boy from P.R. But looking at them, Alicia wondered whether their tension stemmed from something else entirely. Could it be that Jamie and Gaz were always fussing because, deep down inside, Jamie wasn't really the tough New Yorker she pretended to be, and Gaz's memories of Puerto Rico weren't as sweet as he claimed?

"Tell me about your village in Puerto Rico," Jamie said, intent on having the last word. "Have they even paved the roads yet?"

Alicia could see that the jab had gotten to Gaz. "You better cool it, Jamie," she said. "Unless you want to walk home." Then, turning to Gaz, she said, "Don't pay her any attention. I like your ride." Which was really code for "I like *you*," but she and Gaz didn't roll like that. Not yet, anyway, she added to herself. So she waved to her friends and started walking across the circular driveway back toward the front door. She had planning to do and parents to convince. It looked as if the summer would be anything but relaxing.

Sunday morning, Alicia woke up to the sound of her parents leaving for church. She walked into the living room and opened the sliding doors. When her parents were home, the air-conditioning was always on full blast. But Alicia liked the fresh air—even on days like this one, when what little air was circulating was impossibly hot and sticky. She also didn't mind the bugs. Whenever her mother caught her like this, a thin film of sweat covering her face as she absentmindedly swatted away mosquitoes, she said that Alicia was "tropical, heart and soul."

Alicia was wearing one of her mom's old Missoni dresses that she'd cut so that the wavy knit fabric hit just above her knees. She'd cinched it with a wide purple patent-leather belt that emphasized her tiny waist and showed off her hips. Kicking off her purple leather flip-flops, she sat down in her favorite chair with her ideas notebook. Even if it ended up that she couldn't start her *quince* business, she was still determined to hook Sarita up.

An hour later, Alicia looked at her watch, then at her still blank notebook. It was a good thing that Carmen, Gaz, and Jamie would be coming over. She needed help.

The first thing Gaz wanted to know when he arrived was, "Where's my sweetheart Maribelle?"

Alicia laughed. "Down, boy. Today's her day off."

"So, what are we going to have for lunch?" Gaz asked, looking nothing short of forsaken. "No offense, Lici, but half the reason I come to your house is because nobody cooks like Maribelle."

"Yeah, I know we're here to talk business," said Jamie. "But I am a creative person, and I need food to be inspired."

"Me, too," said Carmen. "And I don't do my best work over regular old takeout."

Alicia walked over to the huge Sub-Zero fridge in the kitchen. "Y'all know you're spoiled, right?" she said.

"And?" Jamie said, spinning on a mahogany bar stool.

"*And* it's a good thing that Maribelle left us a crispy calamari salad with hearts of palm, banana, and chayote. Calamari's on the side, so that it stays crisp. And . . ."

She reached for the fridge, but Gaz beat her to it. "Maribelle's homemade sesame-orange dressing," he said, letting out a sigh of happiness.

He dipped a finger into the bottle of salad dressing. "You guys think I'm kidding when I say that I want Maribelle to marry me, but I'm not," he said. "This woman's food is out of this world. She and me could be the next Ashton and Demi."

"She and I, you moron," said Jamie.

"Don't hate, appreciate," Gaz retorted.

"That doesn't even make sense," said Jamie.

"*Si no fueras tonta sería completamente claro,*" Gaz said.

"Oh, here we go with the Spanish," said Jamie, as if Gaz had dealt a particularly low blow.

Of all three of the girls, Jamie spoke the least amount of

Spanish: meaning, none. Her parents had been born in the Bronx and were of the generation that had never bothered to learn; the grandparents spoke the language, then the parents didn't, and then their kids—kids like Jamie, Carmen, Alicia—made varying attempts to learn.

Carmen took a seat at the dining room table and began looking over the sketches Alicia had finally made—minutes before her friends' arrival. They were seriously lacking. *"Chica,"* she said, "tell me you have a better plan for Sarita's *quince* than—are those alien?—*chambelanes*. Otherwise, this business won't even have a chance."

Alicia grinned, handing Carmen a plate of calamari salad and sitting down next to her. "What? I was thinking outside the box. But you're right. It's a terrible idea." She sighed. "I just wish my parents could be as supportive of my planning this *quince* as they are of anything college-related. To them, the thought of the business is horrible."

"Well, what do you expect?" Gaz said. "Your parents are mad successful. They want you to be a big shot, too. If I had someone who could open doors for me at the record companies, I'd jump at the chance."

"And if I had a crib like this and a closet full of clothes like yours, I'd never complain the way you do," Jamie said.

"I'm not complaining, I'm just saying that my parents don't get how important being a Latina is to me," Alicia said, correcting her. "All they really want is that I go to Harvard and get a law degree, which is what they did. You wouldn't understand, Jamie."

Jamie looked hurt, then angry. "Why? Because my parents didn't go to college? Because they didn't go to Harvard?"

"That's not what I meant," Alicia said.

"Of course you did. You're extra, *chica*. I'm used to it by now," Jamie said.

Alicia blanched. Even though she knew that Jamie was just jerking her chain, it was always a short leap between someone inferring that her parents were snobs and sellouts to her feeling like a sellout herself.

"You know it's not like that," Alicia said. "It's just, for some Latinos, they feel like they pulled themselves up by their bootstraps and that everybody should do the same."

"Oh! So starting your own business isn't good enough?" Jamie said.

"*Cállate*, Jamie," Carmen said, holding up one hand. "Stop ripping on Alicia's parents when we're in their house, eating their food—"

"Maribelle's food," Gaz said, as he helped himself to a giant bowl of homemade rice pudding.

Carmen, who was sitting next to him, dipped her spoon into the pudding and continued, "Eating the food that *they* paid for. If Alicia's parents are really dead set against her doing this and the internship, maybe we'll just have to wait and start our *quince* business next summer."

The room grew quiet as everyone finished eating, Carmen's—and Jamie's—words ringing in their ears. Finally, Alicia got up from the table and started to clear the plates. She scraped the uneaten food into the compost can and then began to load the dishwasher in silence.

"Come on, *Boca Grande*," Gaz said to Jamie. "Apologize, so we can all move on with our lives."

She began to protest, but Carmen gave her a look that stopped her cold.

"Okay, fine, whatever," said Jamie, turning to face Alicia. "I'm sorry that I stated the obvious and offended you all by being up-front."

"Maybe we should go," Gaz said.

"What about Sarita's *quince*?" Jamie asked.

"What about it?" Carmen said. "Do you really care?"

Alicia still hadn't said a word. She was rinsing glasses slowly and carefully, as if one clumsy move would make everything shatter to pieces.

"Hey, I'm sorry," Jamie said again, as she walked to the door. "But you shouldn't be so sensitive."

"Te hablo más tarde," Gaz said to Alicia, reaching for his keys.

A subdued "okay" was all that Alicia could manage.

Carmen lingered behind Gaz and Jamie. "I'll stay here

with you," she said gently. "I can take a bus later, or my mom will come pick me up."

"You don't have to," Alicia said.

"I know I don't have to, but I want to," Carmen said, wiping down the counter. Alicia smiled. At least she had Carmen.

When the kitchen was clean enough to meet Maribelle's standards, Alicia and Carmen poured themselves huge glasses of papaya punch and went out to the pool.

"Don't stress, it's not even worth it," Carmen said, getting comfortable on her lounge chair. "It's like, every once in a while, Jamie's got to prove how Bronx she is, so she starts to act like a pissed-off homegirl."

"I don't really think it's her that's making me so upset," Alicia said, shrugging. "It's more that Sarita's *quince* has brought up all this stuff between me and my mom. I always felt like my mom thought having a *quince* was too *ethnic* or something. Then, the other morning, my dad told me that my mom hates *quinces* because, when she was my age, she was too poor to have one. Then Jamie gets in my face about how we're so rich, when I know that my parents used to be really, really poor. It just feels like one big mess."

"It's not a mess," Carmen said. "Your family is a Latino success story. That's something to be *proud* of, not something to be ashamed of. My mom always says no one handed us anything; what we've got, we worked for. That's as true of your family as it is of mine."

Alicia let the words sink in. Carmen was, of course, right.

"And what about this stupid internship?" Alicia said.

"It's not stupid, you're working for the Office of Film and Cultural Affairs. That's awesome. It could actually lead to something. So, stop complaining, before I take Jamie's side."

Alicia felt tears pressing against her eyelids. "What if my mom's right? What if, in trying to do everything, I *fail* at everything?" she asked, choking back the tears.

"Alicia the Talented, you're good at everything! You'll be good at this, too," Carmen said reassuringly. "Besides, you can't quit the internship until you find some cute guys for us to date. That's a perk of working in government, right? And needless to say, I'm meeting no one in the women's department at Saks."

Carmen lay back in her chair and closed her eyes. "Alicia, what if you met some cute young politician, got married, and lived happily ever after? Wouldn't that be magical? Would you name your first child after me?"

"Married? At fifteen? My first child? Is that how they do it in *el campo*, in Mexico?"

"Don't dis Mexico!" Carmen said, getting up. Kneeling by the pool she scooped up water with her hands to splash

Alicia.

"Oh, so you want to play dirty?" Alicia said. "You know we Cubans aren't afraid of a little water. We're just ninety miles from home, baby."

Smiling devilishly, Alicia pushed Carmen—who was fully clothed—into the water. Carmen gasped, then erupted in giggles. Alicia, also fully clothed, quickly jumped in after her. And for the first time since Jamie's hurtful remarks and her fight with her mom, Alicia felt as if things were back to normal.

CHAPTER 5

ALICIA WAS in the kitchen later that night when she heard her mother's voice calling from the garage: "Anybody home?"

"Just me," Alicia called back. She had spent the rest of the afternoon hanging with Carmen, until she left to babysit her younger sisters. Then she'd run on the treadmill for a bit, showered, and changed into her favorite pair of Juicy Couture sweats.

"How was your day?" her mother asked, walking into the kitchen. As always, Mrs. Cruz looked stylish—even when working on a Sunday. She was dressed in a sleeveless burgundy dress and matching jacket. She kicked off her charcoal gray Jimmy Choo kitten heels; Alicia said a quick prayer that her mom would not scuff the Choos up before she passed them down to her.

"Okay," Alicia said. "Carmen came over to swim." She didn't mention the *quince*, Gaz, or the argument she had had with Jamie.

"That's nice," her mother said. She paused and reached for a wineglass. "Sweetie, I'm sorry that I was so angry the other night."

"I'm sorry, too, Mom," Alicia said sincerely.

"I just want what's best for you, Lici. I want you to have everything I never had."

"Like a *quince*?" Alicia regretted the words the moment she said them.

Her mother poured herself a glass of wine, took a sip, and sighed. "Like whatever you want," she said.

"I know," Alicia said, "and I actually do *enjoy* the internship. I'm grateful for everything you and Dad have done for me."

"Who the heck are we, the Brady Bunch?" her brother asked as he breezed into the kitchen, interrupting the moment.

It was a well-known fact that Alex Cruz was genetically gifted. While Alicia was five feet four inches tall on a good day, Alex was over six feet. In hot weather, Alicia's hair was often a dark mop of loco curls. Alex's hair was dark blond, and he wore it long and surfer shaggy, as if he were always six weeks behind with his haircut appointments. The siblings were both creative, though. Alicia had her dancing, and Alex was a genius at building things. He was the kid who took apart the waffle maker to see how it worked, then put it together just like new.

He and Alicia were only eighteen months apart, and even though the touchy-feely thing was not big in the Cruz household—hence Alex's joke about the Brady Bunch—Alicia and her brother were close. For as long as she could remember, he had always been by her side. Whether she was learning how to ride a bike, flying on a plane for the first time, or attending her first day at C. G. High, she would always catch, out of the corner of her eye, a glimpse of her brother's hair, the Lacoste shirts that were his uniform, a flash of his sideways smile. It was comforting.

"Don't let me interrupt the mamapalooza," Alex said. "It's just that I'm starvin' like Marvin. Can somebody holler when Dad gets home and we're ready to eat?"

He reached for an apple and headed for the Florida room.

"Don't eat, it'll ruin your appetite," his mother said, on autopilot.

Alex turned and smiled. "Don't eat this *very* healthy apple because I'm a *growing* boy and I *crave* my fruits and vegetables?"

"*Vaya,*" his mother said, shooing him away. "Your father will be home soon."

"So," Alicia said, again eyeing her mother's Jimmy Choos. "If I'm going to work at City Hall, then I'm going to need to get some grown-up clothes. Or borrow some stuff from you.

For example, those shoes you were wearing today . . ."

"Ha, *niña*," her mother said, "you do this internship, you go to Harvard, you go to law school, then maybe we'll talk about me buying you some outrageously expensive designer shoes. For now, help me with dinner."

They had just put the *pernil* in the oven when Alicia's father came home from playing tennis.

"What's the *qué pasa*?" he said, tugging on Alicia's ponytail.

Then he walked over to her mother and kissed her full on the mouth. *"Hola, mi amor,"* he whispered to his wife.

"Consider me officially grossed out," Alicia said, mostly because they expected her to. But she liked it that her parents still kissed. Some of her friends had *such* complicated family lives. Carmen's dad, Javier, had remarried: a blond *cubana* named Natalia, who was only nine years older than Carmen's eldest sister. Carmen's mom, Sophia, was now married to Christian, an Anglo history professor at the local college. But Carmen also spent time with Mariella, who was her father's first wife—her mother was her father's second wife, and Natalia was his third. Mariella rented the guest house from Carmen's dad and was like a second mother to Carmen, who liked to say, *"Es un pocito confundido.* A little confusing." Her affectionate—even if kind of gross to Alicia—parents were at least *less* confusing.

"Alex!" Alicia screamed. "*Papi's* home!"

"Call me when the food's on the table! I'm watching the soccer game!" Alex yelled back from the living room.

"No," Alicia said. "Come help me set the table."

"It's four plates, four forks, four knives," Alex said, coming to stand at the kitchen door. "You can't possibly need help with that."

"Help your sister," their father said, tossing his jacket over a kitchen bar stool. When the table was set, the family sat down to eat.

"Alicia, your mother and I have talked about it," her father said after he had taken a few bites of food, "and it's fine for you to help your friend plan her *quince* as long as you understand that your internship comes first."

Alicia tried not to jump out of her seat. This was great news—no, make that fantastic news!

"Do not embarrass your father at his job," her mother added.

"Never!" Alicia replied, thinking that even if her father hadn't been the deputy mayor there was no way that Lori, the wicked witch of South Beach, would let her slack off on the internship. She would show her parents that she could handle this—she hoped.

After dinner, Alicia jumped up from the table. "I've got to go call Sarita, and Carmen and Jamie and Gaz; then I'll come back and load the dishwasher, promise!" She couldn't wait to tell everyone the good news.

"I got it," Alex said with a wink. "It's only four plates, four forks, and four knives. It's not exactly a two-person job."

Alicia gave her brother a quick hug and said, "Thanks for having my back."

"Always," he said.

And although she rarely thought about how much she leaned on her big brother, Alicia was glad to hear him say it. He did have her back, and that felt good. It wasn't every girl who was cool with her seventeen-year-old brother. She smiled. And it wasn't every girl who got to plan *quinceañeras*—as a job!

The next weekend, Alicia gathered the Amigas at Lario's on Miami Beach for their first official meeting since her parents had given the okay. She was so excited she'd arrived ten minutes early. She'd dressed in her new favorite outfit: a one-shoulder black blouse, a pair of boot-cut white jeans, and a pair of worn Chanel sandals that her mom had given to her. The sandals were a little torn, but the double C's always made Alicia feel extra grown-up.

She asked for a table for five, and as she waited for the rest of the group to arrive, she laid out all the materials she'd prepared. There were so many details of a *quince* to work out. No wonder so many moms went a bit loco with the planning. But if she and her friends could make Sarita's party completely cool and completely unforgettable, then all of Miami would look to them for *quince* planning, and they would have themselves a legitimate business.

Carmen came in soon after Alicia, looking fabulous in a red sundress with a bubble skirt.

"Hola, loca," she said, giving Alicia a *besito* on the cheek. She sat down at the table and took a sketch pad out of her World Food Program bag.

"I'm so excited about designing my first *quince* dress," Carmen said. She took out an ad for DiaNoches, a fancy boutique in Coral Gables that specialized in *quince* dresses. The owner of DiaNoches also happened to be Simone Baldonado's mom. "Have you seen this?" Carmen asked.

"Nope, but it's good research, right?" Alicia said, flipping through the pages.

"Hardly," Carmen scoffed. "It's one poufy dress after another. These girls don't look like *quinces*, they look like plastic wedding-cake toppers!"

Alicia laughed. "Look at this one! I feel like the hosts of that show *What Not to Wear*. These girls are serious fashion victims, in need of help that only we can provide."

Jamie arrived and took a seat next to Carmen.

"So, what's up?" Jamie said to Alicia. Then she added, "Nice outfit."

"Thanks," Alicia said, with a small smile. She knew what

Jamie was doing. She was trying to make amends, but she was never actually going to apologize. That was typical Jamie.

When Gaz slid into the booth, Alicia let out a breath. He had a way of easing tension—spoken or unspoken. A moment later, a waiter came. He took their drink orders, then asked if they were ready to order food.

"We should probably wait for our client to arrive," Alicia told him.

Jamie couldn't resist the opportunity to get in a dig. "Client?" she said. "Oh, is that what you call a fourteen-year-old girl who wants a *quince*?"

Alicia was steamed. "Duh. That's what a *quince* business is—helping fourteen-year-old girls plan parties of legendary proportions. And yes," she added to her friends, "we can call her a client, because we are doing this! With parents on board, Amigas Incorporated is now open for business."

"Yeah, and what's up with dissing the fourteen-year-olds?" Carmen asked.

Because she was so tall, so mature-looking, and such a fantastic seamstress, it was easy for them to forget that Carmen had skipped the second grade. And even though they had all just finished the tenth grade, she was only fourteen, a year younger than Alicia and Jamie. Gaz, on the other hand, was sixteen. His English hadn't been that great when his family came to the U.S., and his mother had decided to let him repeat a grade so he could catch up.

"Okay, try this on for size," Gaz said to Jamie. "*Cállate*. Be really nice to Alicia or you quit the club. We're all still friends, we can all chill, but if you don't respect her vision, then you oughtta bounce. She's working really hard to pull this all together."

Jamie looked as if she were about to make a comment about Alicia's "vision," but a stern glare from Gaz stopped her in her tracks.

"Are you in or out?" Gaz said.

"I'm in," Jamie said. "You guys know how I am. I'm quick to speak my mind, but I'm always down for my peeps."

"Apology accepted," Alicia said with a wink. She didn't want to fight anymore and knew that the implied apology was all she was going to get.

Just then, Sarita arrived. She was dressed in a zebra-print halter top, black shorts, and black gladiator sandals.

"Hey, y'all, sorry I'm late," she said, taking the seat next to Alicia. After introductions had been made, she went on: "My mom is so psyched that we're going to get some help in the *quince* planning. But she wants to know how much this is all going to cost. We've got a five-thousand-dollar budget, but we hadn't thought we'd be paying a party-planner, too. So I want to make sure I can afford you guys."

"*No te preocupes,*" Alicia said, her mind still reeling at the huge number Sarita had given. "Since you're the first official client of Amigas Incorporated, we are going to do your *quince* completely for free. The only thing the budget will pay for are things we have to buy."

"Fabulous!" Sarita said. "Let's get this party started. *Vamos a echar la casa por la ventana.*"

Gaz burst out laughing. "That's what I'm talking about," he said, reaching across the table to give Sarita a high five.

Alicia, Carmen, and Jamie looked confused.

"Translation, please," Alicia finally said.

"Oh, I'm sorry," Sarita said sweetly. "I assumed you spoke Spanish."

Alicia figured there was no real value in faking the funk. "I speak a little Spanish and a lot of Spanglish," she said, sheepishly.

"*Yo también,*" Carmen said.

Jamie was uncharacteristically silent.

"So, what was that thing you said?" Alicia asked.

"*Vamos a echar la casa por la ventana?*" Sarita said. "It means, 'We're going to throw the house out of the window.'"

"And that means—?" Jamie asked.

"It's Mexican for 'the roof, the roof, the roof is on fire,'" Gaz said, winking at Sarita.

"So, what's the plan for my *quince*?" Sarita asked, getting back on topic.

"Well, first and foremost," Alicia said. "You need a theme. A theme is what makes a *quince* hot."

"Or not," Jamie added.

"And while Amigas is brand-new," Alicia said, "rest assured, there is one kind of *quince* we don't do. . . ."

"Princess *quinces*!" Alicia, Carmen, and Jamie said in unison.

"That's a shame," Sarita said, feigning disappointment. "Because I . . . am *nobody's* princess."

"What are you into?" Gaz asked, trying to stay on track.

Sarita shrugged. "Well, I love reggaeton."

"That's music, not a theme," Jamie said, reaching across the table for the pitcher of horchata that the waitress had left at their request.

"And I *love* Cuban food," Sarita said.

"That's catering, not a theme," Carmen said, passing around a plate of steaming hot sweet *platanos* that were fresh from the pan.

"I'm starting to think that maybe being a princess isn't so bad," Sarita said.

"No, we can do better than princess," Alicia said. "You're really into environmentalism, right? We could do a green *quince*."

Everyone at the table made a slightly disgusted face.

"I'm not a girl, so maybe my opinion doesn't count," Gaz

said. "But something about a green *quince* makes me think about leprechauns and . . ."

"Green horchatas," Jamie added.

"And a green *quince* cake," Carmen said, sticking her tongue out. "Yuck."

"Y'all are being way too literal," Alicia said.

The waitress put down a huge platter of pressed sandwiches and for a moment, there was silence as everyone tucked in, their mouths full of ham, pickles, grainy mustard, and melted cheese.

Finally Sarita spoke. "You know, the thing is that environmentalism is really just my gateway hobby."

"What's that even mean?" Jamie asked.

"It means that I want to protect the ozone layer, because I need it to be there for me to break through it."

Carmen raised an eyebrow. "Please explain."

"I plan on studying rocket science so I can travel on a spaceship for NASA someday," Sarita said matter-of-factly. "It's the only thing I've ever wanted to do with my life. I love everything about outer space."

Alicia smiled. "That's pretty cool. I'm impressed." She was busy writing in her notebook but suddenly looked up and said, "That's *it*, Sarita. You should have a space-themed *quince*."

"It would be different," Gaz said.

"Different is good," Carmen said, encouragingly.

"Except when it's not," Jamie countered.

"Come on, guys," Alicia said. "When are we not fabulous? We can do this."

Alicia put her ideas notebook in the middle of the table and began drawing. "Picture this. A stage covered in silver balloons, to represent the surface of the moon. The backdrop is black, with the Milky Way galaxy shown in detail."

Alicia showed Sarita the quick sketches.

"It's beautiful," Sarita said.

"Stage right, we have a silver rocket," Alicia went on.

"But not made out of tinfoil," Sarita said. "Because that would be so tacky."

"Don't worry," Carmen said. "We don't do tacky."

Alicia shook her head. "No, we don't. A silver rocket, made by my genius brother," Alicia said. "Most definitely not made of tinfoil.

"We hook you up to a harness, and instead of descending from a platform, like some *quinces* do," Alicia went on, "you're lying flat on the ground, beneath the balloons. Then we lift you with the harness, because there's zero gravity on the moon."

"And maybe we do sort of a reveal," Carmen suggested, growing excited. "You're dressed in a white lab coat in the beginning, with thick black horn-rimmed glasses—like a scientist." She grabbed Alicia's notebook and made a quick sketch. "Then we lift you into the air, and, backstage, you ditch the robe and the glasses, to reveal something like this," she went on. She had drawn a beautiful minidress with diamond-shaped sequins across the bodice.

"See, the sequins are kind of like stars in the night sky, but subtle," she explained. "And it could be silver tulle, to give it a lighter-than-air look."

"Me encanta," Sarita said. She had a "pinch me, I must be dreaming" grin on her face. "*This* is the hotness. Can I take the sketch to show my mom? She's going to freak."

"Uh-oh," Carmen chimed in.

"No, I mean, freak in a good way," Sarita said.

Carmen took out her colored pencils and quickly copied what she had drawn earlier. "Here," she said, handing Sarita the page. "This one's for you."

"I love it," Sarita said. Then she glanced at her watch. "But I'd better go. My mom is picking me up at two, and I want to run into the store next door before she comes. So, what's next?"

"We've only got four weeks until your *quince,* which is, by the way, bananas," Alicia said, smiling. "You'll meet with me first, and we'll make a checklist of all the details. Carmen will start fitting your dress, and we'll start dance rehearsals."

"Don't forget, we've got to talk about hair and makeup," Jamie said. "How do you feel about extensions?"

Sarita shrugged. "I'm kind of on the short side. Do you think they'd look good?"

"You'd look good in anything," Carmen said. "And let's not forget invitations. As soon as we secure the venue, Jamie will make you the most amazing handmade invitations. We've got to get those out as soon as possible. We don't have that much time."

"*Fantástico,*" Sarita said. "Who would've thought that I could move to Miami and less than a month later meet a posse of cool girls who would help me plan my *quince.*"

"Hey, I'm not a girl," Gaz protested.

"No arguments there," Sarita said, winking as she got up to leave.

When Sarita was gone, Gaz excused himself and went to the restroom.

"Does everyone in the world have a crush on Gaz?" Carmen asked those who remained at the table.

"Well there is someone here who definitely does," Jamie said, looking over Alicia's head and pretending to speak exclusively to Carmen. She smiled slyly. "Alicia is, like, this undercover, shy girl. Loud, friendly, the life of the party, but she won't tell one of her best friends that she has feelings for him."

"Hello! Sitting right here," Alicia said.

"Tell him," Carmen urged. "We don't have boyfriends, but *you* don't have to be single."

"What if he doesn't like me back?" Alicia asked in a serious tone. "Then I'll have ruined a perfectly good friendship."

"Trust me, he likes you back," Carmen said.

Gaz reappeared and caught the tail end of the conversation. "Who likes who back?"

"Jamie," Alicia said, her cheeks turning bright red. "She's crushing on this guy at work."

That, she thought, had been too close.

CHAPTER 6

ON MONDAY, Alicia brought the album of pictures from her *quince* trip in to work to show Sarita. Apart from their coffee runs for Lori and occasional trips to the copy machine, they were getting no internship work done. They spent the entire day talking *quinceañera*.

Alicia was surprised at how much she enjoyed telling Sarita about the way she'd spent her fifteenth. "My parents said I could bring a friend, so I invited Carmen to join us."

Alicia explained that her birthday had been on December 16 and that they had left for Spain the day after Christmas. She and Carmen had laughed and gossiped throughout the plane ride over. They'd watched *Flashdance* on Alicia's portable DVD player, and then they'd watched *Ocean's Eleven*, because it was Carmen's favorite flick.

Alicia told Sarita how in Barcelona, they had hung out every evening on the Rambla, the big main street that had a huge sidewalk down the middle with all kinds of performers, cafés, and flower shops.

"It's like something out of a movie," Sarita said, looking through the photos. "You look like Penélope Cruz in *Vicky Cristina Barcelona*."

"Well, I hope I'm not that crazy!" Alicia said.

"You know what I mean, and *fíjase!* the boys in these pictures are so-o-o-o-o cute!" Sarita giggled.

Alicia explained that she and Carmen had a blast pretending to be from Spain—no small feat, since their Spanish was busted. But if they just listened to a guy speak and threw in a *"vale, vale"* every once in a while—the Spanish equivalent of "yep"—then they could fool the boys for a little while.

In Spain, dinner was never served before nine in the evening, even on a weeknight, which meant that Alicia's curfew had been automatically extended. Her parents let her and Carmen sit on their own in restaurants and cafés, and everyone thought they were way older than they actually were. They spent New Year's Eve at a tapas bar located in an old bullfighting ring. Right before the clock struck midnight, their waiter handed them all a bunch of grapes and said that if they ate twelve before the final chime, then all their wishes for the new year would come true. Alicia wolfed down the grapes, dreaming about Gaz and Harvard and some really fierce Gucci boots.

That had been the trip of a lifetime. It had been fun to learn a little more Spanish. But the experience hadn't felt steeped in family and history and culture, the way some of the *quinces* she had attended did. She tried to remember whether she and her mother had ever really discussed having a *quince*. She recalled her mother saying something like, "You don't want a big, nightmare *quince* with a pink poufy dress and all your guy cousins dressed up as *chambelanes*." To which Alicia had, of course, replied, "No way."

But had they ever talked about what *quinces* meant historically? Had they ever discussed whether there was a way for Alicia to have a *quince* that was modern and interesting and that reflected her personal style? Alicia didn't think so, and there was a part of her that wished she'd at least *explored* the possibilities before taking the trip instead.

All the memories and what-ifs suddenly overwhelmed her. "Excuse me; bathroom run," she said, handing the album to Sarita.

The minute Alicia locked the stall door behind her, the tears came and wouldn't stop. She knew that there was a part of her that envied Sarita for the chance to do a splashy *quince* with a cool-girl twist. Somehow, the further the Spain trip receded in time, the more Alicia doubted her choice not to have a *quince*. But there was no turning back. Alicia was never going to have another fifteenth birthday again. And the more she thought about it, the harder she cried.

• • •

The next day, when Sarita came in to the office, she was surprised to find Carmen sitting at her desk, behind several yards of billowing material. Alicia was standing next to her, a smile on her face.

"Hey, girl," Alicia sang out. She was wearing a pink and white wrap dress and looked as if she'd been bright-eyed and bushy-tailed for hours—something Sarita was beginning to realize was standard for her. "Time to fit your dress," Alicia said.

Sarita, for her part, had spent the night doing a 24 marathon with her mom and was more than a little sleepy. Now her fuzzy brain was trying to take everything in. "Here?" she asked, looking around at the busy office.

"Well, not here, exactly," Alicia said cheerfully. "Use the bathroom."

Sarita seemed nervous. "I'm not sure Lori would approve."

"Don't worry," Alicia said. "I've got your back. You and Carmen can go to the third-floor bathroom to change." She handed Sarita a key. "You'll need this."

"Are you sure we won't get in trouble?" Sarita asked.

"What trouble?" Alicia said. "I'll make sure Lori gets her bi-hourly cup of Joe, and anyway, what's she going to do to me? My father's the deputy mayor. She can't fire me." The moment the words came out of her mouth, Alicia regretted them. She'd come across just the way she had never wanted to sound: like a rich, spoiled brat.

"You know what I mean," she said, backpedaling. "This is an awesome internship, and I would never want to jeopardize it. But they're only so many hours in the day, your *quince* is a month away, we're going to have to start doing some of the planning here at work."

Shooing the girls out the door, Alicia got Lori her cup of coffee. Then she dashed to the third-floor bathroom, where Carmen and Sarita were waiting. The floor was dominated by estate-planning offices, and with so many people handling their requests via e-mail, it was almost always empty.

"Let's get this fabric on you," Carmen said.

Sarita was both nervous and excited. "Look at me," she said, stretching out her trembling hand. "I'm shaking! I have no idea why."

Carmen wrapped the fabric around her. And it could've been simply the way the light came through the window, but all three girls inhaled sharply when Sarita twirled around. The fabric practically glowed, and it was easy to imagine Sarita's wearing it at the church ceremony. She'd look . . . angelic.

"You're going to be a vision, *niña*," Alicia said, lifting a hand to her heart.

"I love it," Sarita said. "I'm going to cry."

"Don't cry! You'll mess up the fabric," Carmen pleaded.

"Hmm," Alicia said, circling around her, a questioning expression on her face. "Let's talk about length."

Carmen took out her pins. "I was thinking that just below the knee would be sweet but not stodgy."

Alicia crossed her arms. "No, I think it should be longer."

Carmen pinned the temporary hemline so that it grazed Sarita's toes.

Alicia looked dissatisfied. "That's no good. Shorter."

Carmen pinned it at the ankle.

"No, even shorter," Alicia said.

Carmen practically growled. "This is where we started, *loca*."

"Longer," Alicia said.

Carmen pinned.

"Now shorter," Alicia said.

Carmen adjusted the hemline again.

"Too short!" Alicia said.

"You know what? I'm done," Carmen said, standing up and unpinning Sarita. "The length was perfect the first time."

Alicia stood there silently. She knew this was one battle she had to let go. "Carmen's right, as usual," she said, yielding.

• • •

Later that night, as she rode the bus home, Alicia became lost in thought. Her father's words, *There's always a third way: your way, my way, or the third way, compromise,* echoed through her mind. The situation with Carmen was the perfect example.

Alicia took out her phone and texted Carmen: *One dress down, one dress to go.*

Carmen would probably finish the formal white dress for the ceremony itself in a day. But she still had to create the fun dress for dinner and dancing afterward.

Then Alicia sent a second message: *Carmen, sorry if I was a little bossy today. You know how I am. I can be a little OTP. I know the dresses you are designing will be SO, SO BEAUTIFUL.*

Carmen texted back: *No problem,* chica. *Just don't make it a habit. It's the* Amigas Club. *Not the* Divas Club.

CHAPTER 7

THAT SATURDAY, Alicia and Gaz met up to find a location for Sarita's *quince*. It was one of the most important things on the to-do list, but between her internship and Gaz's job, it had been hard to find the time. They needed to get this settled.

"Okay," Alicia said, getting into Gaz's car. "First stop, the Miami Science Museum. I haven't been there since I was a kid, but I spoke to a lady over the phone who said that they've got a planetarium where all of Sarita's guests can view a U2 stargazing show, then move into a party room."

"Cool, let's hit it," Gaz said.

Alicia turned on the radio, and immediately a CD started playing. She didn't recognize it, but she liked it.

"This is really good," she said. "Who is it?"

"It's me," Gaz said.

"Stop messing around," Alicia said, surprised. "I've heard you put a hurting on Ricky Martin at the karaoke spot, but I never heard you sound like this."

Gaz smiled. "Don't hate on 'La Vida Loca'—it's a classic."

"So is 'Hips Don't Lie,'" Alicia said. "But that doesn't make me Shakira."

"I don't know about that," Gaz said. "I've seen you dance. You can swivel those hips with the best of them."

Alicia could feel her face getting hot. Gaz had never said anything about her hips—or any other part of her body, for that matter—before. She wanted to push him further, but she couldn't think of anything sexy to say.

"So, tell me about this CD," she said, moving the subject back into more manageable territory.

"It's a new sound I've been working on with my brothers," Gaz said. "Dez plays guitar. Esteban plays bass, and Carlos is like a modern-day Tito Puente. If it's a percussion instrument, he can play it. But you already knew that."

"I keep telling you you should promote your music more," Alicia said, nodding. "Sarita's *quince* could be huge for you guys. You're going to be so amazing!"

Gaz suddenly looked shy. "I don't know."

"Why?" Alicia said.

"I don't know," Gaz repeated, staring straight ahead. "Playing in my garage is one thing. Strangers is totally different." He needed a haircut, and there was a curl that kept looping over the right side of his face. Alicia had to fight the impulse to push it behind his ear.

He looks so darn cute, she thought. Wearing a Gap (Product) Red T and faded blue jeans, he was like the quint-essential Miami hottie. He had his window rolled down, his car had nothing that even *resembled* air-conditioning, and still Alicia thought his face looked beautiful. As they drove on the main interstate, right along the beach, and she could catch glimpses of blue behind the profile view of his eyes, his ears, his lips . . .

Alicia snapped out of the total daze into which she had fallen. "You've got to put together a set list," she said, trying to cover.

Gaz gave her a strange look. "I was just telling you I had. Where's your head, Cruz?"

Alicia quickly realized that he must've told her while she had been daydreaming about him. "Good," she said. "Really good. I mean, thanks."

"I'm the one who should be thanking you," Gaz said. "And Amigas. I'm a little shy about my music, but if I want it to succeed, I've got to put it out there."

Being back at the museum brought up all kinds of memories for Alicia. She'd forgotten how majestic the main lobby was, with its ceiling that seemed to go right up to the heavens, and the skeleton of a giant dinosaur, reconstructed from real dinosaur bones. She could picture the limo pulling up to the museum and Sarita and her date walking up the museum's big stone steps. Add to that the planetarium show, and once they'd tricked out the party room, this was going to be a *quinceañera* that no one in Miami would ever forget.

At the main desk, Alicia asked for Ms. Seager, the director of events.

A few minutes later, an elderly woman came out, and the girl at the information booth pointed her toward Alicia and Gaz.

"Well, hello, there," the woman said. "Nice to meet you." Ms. Seager was dressed in a bright pink Lilly Pulitzer dress, and her back was hunched over in a way that suggested she could not have straightened up even if she had wanted to.

"You, too," Alicia said, reaching out to shake the woman's hand. "We spoke on the phone."

"Yes, yes," Ms. Seager said. "And this must be your husband."

Gaz raised an eyebrow. "Yes, I must."

Alicia wanted to die. If there were a God, he would have opened up the lobby floor and had her sucked into a different dimension. Couldn't Ms. Seager see that she was only fifteen? And that Gaz was only sixteen? And that they were certainly *not* married? Alicia looked at the woman, who wore startlingly thick glasses, and realized that chances were good that she couldn't see much of anything. Still, she thought, she'd better set the record straight.

"This is Gaz Fuentes," Alicia said. "He's my business partner."

"How sweet! Married and working together, too," the woman said. "And you have a little girl, and you're planning a party for her, right?"

Alicia was about to correct her when Gaz, who was clearly quite amused by the scenario, shook his head. *Why bother?* he mouthed.

Alicia gave in. How could she resist? "We'd like to see the planetarium room and the party space," she said.

"Excellent," Ms. Seager answered. "Follow me. I'll take you up in the staff elevator. I've worked here for fifty-two years, and it still gives me a thrill."

Alicia and Gaz followed her down a long hallway of offices, then into the staff elevators. They exchanged a glance, clearly thinking the same thing. The old lady was a little batty, but going behind the scenes at a museum was really cool.

Ms. Seager took them into the planetarium room, which was a good-size auditorium, with a massive, pale blue, domed ceiling. The major constellations—the Big Dipper, the Little Dipper, and Orion—were painted across it in gold. It was stunning.

"We project the film up there," Ms. Seager bellowed. "We've even got IMAX."

"This is great," Alicia said, "exactly what we're looking for."

Gaz looked around. "When's the next show? I almost want to stay."

Ms. Seager smiled. "The next show is at three p.m. If you want to stay, I will provide complimentary tickets for you and your lovely wife."

Alicia flushed. She wanted to say something, but Gaz just put his arm around her and said, "My wife and I would love that."

She let out a sigh. Nice of him to turn it into a joke, when he *knew* she had feelings for him.

Of course, she'd never actually said that she had feelings for him.

But he *knew*. He *must*! How could he not know? She never talked about other guys. She spent every weekend with him. What did he think? That she was some kind of nun? She liked him, and if she hadn't been worried about ruining their friendship, she would have said something.

At that very instant, Alicia had a major *Aha* moment. What if Gaz liked her but wasn't saying anything because *he* didn't want to ruin their friendship? How were they ever going to get together? And how could one lousy date ruin five years of friendship? If it was weird, they'd just never date or smooch or make googly eyes again. No big thing.

• • •

"Alicia," Gaz said, shaking her by the shoulder. She had zoned out again. "Ms. Seager's ready to show us the party room."

Then he leaned down and whispered, "And God knows, she is not getting any younger."

Stiffling giggles, they followed her back to the staff elevator, and this time, Ms. Seager pressed the button for the fourth floor.

They walked past the anatomy room and the shark exhibit to a black door behind a kinetics exhibit, consisting of a big glass tank full of golf balls that moved under certain levels of pressure and air.

"This is a very special party space," Ms. Seager said. "I know you're going to love it."

She opened up the door, and Alicia let out a gasp. There were little bitty plastic chairs around an oval-topped table that was covered with a plastic tablecloth with pictures of princesses dressed in pink all over it. The ceiling was painted with blue and white balloons, and in the middle of the room there was a five-foot-long folding screen with life-size *Cinderella* characters painted on either side.

Gaz burst out laughing.

"I thought you said this was a multipurpose party room," Alicia sputtered.

"It is," Ms. Seager said. "When the birthday child is a boy, we put up red and black balloons, and we bring out our

Spider-Man screen. We also do a very exciting experiment with real spiders. The kids *love* it."

"Are there any other party spaces?" Alicia asked, trying hard not to hyperventilate.

"No, my dear," Ms. Seager said. "This is it. It's just been renovated. What's the matter? Do you think your little girl won't like it?"

Alicia had gone to a yoga class with Carmen and her mom once. Right now, she knew she needed to do yoga breaths. But she couldn't remember how to do yoga breaths. She felt as if she were going to pass out. She put a hand against the wall to steady herself. She needed to think. This was the first big hiccup in their planning—and Alicia did not deal well with hiccups.

The planetarium was awesome. Having the *quince* guests arrive in the fancy museum lobby would set just the right tone. The room was a little small, but they could fit the guests in it—maybe. Okay, who was she fooling? Sarita would just have to trim her guest list. Alex would do an awesome set design and it would still be the hotness. Most important, the price was right. Five hundred dollars for the room rental *and* the planetarium show. She could make it work. She *had* to make it work.

"What kind of flexibility do we have with the room?" Alicia asked. "We'd like to bring in a band."

"Oh, no," Ms. Seager said. "We couldn't have that. Too loud. This is a museum, after all."

"How about a DJ?" Gaz asked, trying not to sound too annoyed. "Someone to play records, at a reasonable volume."

Ms. Seager considered the notion. "That may be permissible," she said. "I'd have to look into it."

Alicia smiled thinly. "Okay, so we'd like to reserve the room for six hours. From six p.m. to midnight."

The director let out a giggle. "Midnight! We'd all turn into pumpkins," she said.

Alicia sighed. "Okay, how about six p.m. to eleven p.m.?"

"Oh, no," Ms. Seager said. "That isn't possible, either. There are only two time slots for our birthday bashes, ten a.m. to one p.m., or two p.m. to five p.m. The museum closes at six, and the staff needs ample time to clean up afterward."

The museum closed at six? How had Alicia missed that detail?

"Are there no exceptions? Not even for special occasions?" she asked, her hope fading.

"None whatsoever," Ms. Seager said. "Rules are rules, you know."

Alicia was crushed. She had no plan B, and Sarita's *quince* was only weeks away. "I'm sorry, it's just not going to work," she said softly.

"Oh, I'm sorry to hear that," Ms. Seager said. "I'd still be glad to offer you and your husband tickets to the three p.m. Night Sky show in our planetarium."

"We'd love them," Gaz said.

"We'd love them, but we can't," Alicia said sternly.

Back in the car, Alicia banged her head against Gaz's dashboard.

"Just shoot me," she said.

"No need," Gaz answered. "I have an idea."

"Good," Alicia said. "I want to hear it."

"It's a space-themed *quince*, right?" Gaz said.

Alicia nodded.

"And where do real rockets leave from, right here in Florida?"

"Cape Canaveral," Alicia said. "But that's, like, a six-hour drive away, and I don't even know if they have a party space."

Gaz rolled his eyes. "Sometimes you're just a little slow. Sweet, but slow. *Where* is Cape Canaveral located?"

"Orlando?" Alicia asked. Maybe Gaz was right. Maybe she was slow. Because at this particular moment, she was very, very confused.

"No, Einstein, the beach," Gaz said. "Cape Canaveral is on the beach."

Alicia smiled, finally getting it. "It doesn't cost any money to have a party on the beach."

"You just need a permit," Gaz said.

"And I *do* work at City Hall," Alicia said, grinning. "I love it, Gaz, thank you!"

She threw her arms around him, and maybe it was her imagination, but when he hugged her back, it felt as if he lingered for just a few seconds longer than necessary.

"There's only one problem," Alicia said. "If we have it on the beach, then there's no place to hang the harness for Sarita's astronaut dance."

Gaz turned on the ignition, and they started to drive back to Coral Gables. "I think I know the perfect spot on the beach," he said.

"What about the harness?" Alicia asked. "It's a key element of my choreography."

Gaz gave her a look that said, *You've got to be kidding me.*

"I'm serious," Alicia said. "I want Sarita to have a fly *quince*, but I also want to showcase my choreography. I need a harness."

"Scratch the harness," Gaz said.

"I—," Alicia began, but Gaz cut her off.

"Scratch the harness," he repeated.

"Scratching the harness," Alicia said, settling back into her seat. He was cute. Even when he was being bossy.

CHAPTER 8

THE NEXT day, Alicia met Carmen at her house to work on firming up the checklist and the budget. Carmen's house in South Beach was the very opposite of Alicia's pristine home in the Gables. Carmen's family lived in a 1930s bungalow on the canal facing New River. The bright pink three-bedroom house was in dire need of a paint job, and inside, all the rooms were ramshackle—probably because there were two parents and six kids living there. Carmen lived with her mom, her stepdad, her sister, Una, her brother, Tino, and her three stepsisters, Laura, Lindsay, and Lula.

Una was seventeen and was in Alex's class at C. G. High. Her real name was Valentina. When she was little and people asked her if she wanted brothers or sisters, she would shake her head vehemently and say, "No, *solo una, solo una*," meaning that she wanted to be an only child. And while it was ironic that the girl who wanted to be an only child ended up with five siblings, the nickname Una had stuck.

Tino was sixteen, hot, and a local soccer star. His picture was in the paper regularly. Everyone said that he was going to make it to the pros. Alicia had to admit that she'd spent a good part of junior high crushing on Tino, but she had finally realized that all he was ever going to love, at least for the foreseeable future, was his soccer ball—and the occasional overfriendly cheerleader.

Carmen's stepsisters were the definition of "adorable." They were all blond-haired, blue-eyed versions of Carmen's stepdad, Christian, a history professor who taught at Florida International. He'd come to Miami from England for a vacation after finishing college, fallen in love with the weather, and never left. Laura and Lula were six-year-old twins. Lindsay was eight. Carmen liked to pretend that they got on her nerves, but the L's, as she and Alicia called them, worshipped the ground she walked on, and she loved them to pieces.

"Welcome to the jungle," Carmen said as Alicia entered the front yard.

It wasn't quite a jungle, but the garden *was* overrun with tropical plants and fruit-bearing trees. Fallen mangoes and coconuts were scattered across the lawn. Inside the house, Carmen's mother, Sophia, was sitting at the kitchen table, paying bills. All of Carmen's friends knew Carmen's mom. She was the head of the math department at C. G. High. She was the person you saw if you wanted to place out of the math requirement by taking an algebra test, or if you wanted to take AP trigonometry. Carmen's mom was not just good at numbers. She was also fluent in Italian and Chinese, as well as Spanish.

"Mom, Alicia is here," Carmen said, going to the fridge and getting two bottles of Mexican soda. Alicia loved Jarrito's tamarind-flavored drink and happily took one when Carmen handed it to her.

"How are my favorite entrepreneurs doing?" Sophia asked, giving the girls a smile.

"Great," Alicia said. "Our first client is awesome."

"Now we've just got to confirm our checklist and deal with the budget," Carmen said. "We've been kind of going about this blindly."

"Well," Sophia said, "I was just paying bills, so I've got my calculator out and my budget brain on. Do you want some help?"

"No," Carmen said, her knee-jerk reaction being to turn the parental unit down, no matter what.

"We would love help," Alicia said. "Carmen, we've got a girl's *quince* on our hands, and we've never done this before."

Carmen relented.

"All right, then. Tell me what you've got so far," Sophia said.

Alicia took out her Amigas folder and her ideas notebook.

"Sarita's new in town, and she wants to be an aeronautical engineer," she explained.

"Smart girl," Sophia said.

"And she wants a space-themed *quince*," Carmen added.

"Well, that's unique," Sophia said.

"I've got an idea for an opening dance number and a set," Alicia said. "And Carmen is making the dresses."

"*Claro,*" Sophia said. She herself couldn't sew a single stitch, but Carmen had learned from their neighbor, Senora Olga, who lived across the street and was like a grandmother to Carmen, her brother, and her sisters.

"Gaz will do the music," Alicia went on. "Jamie's on hair, makeup, and invitations."

"This sounds great," Sophia said, visibly impressed. "So, what else?"

"We still need to figure out flowers, a photographer, and a limo," Alicia said.

"What about the venue?" Sophia said. "That seems like it's going to be your biggest expense."

"Well, I'm not too worried. The budget is *huge*," Alicia said. "And the venue—the beach—is cheap!"

"Really?" Sophia asked. "How *huge* a budget are we talking?"

"Five thousand dollars," Alicia replied. "Like I said, this is going to be a *breeze*."

Sophia looked amused. "I hate to be the one to break it

to you, but five thousand dollars isn't a huge budget. It's not tiny, but it's not huge."

"What are you talking about?" Alicia said.

"Do you know how much the average *quinceañera* costs in Miami?" Carmen's mom asked.

Alicia shrugged.

"Between ten thousand and fifteen thousand dollars," said Sophia.

"That's *bananas*!" Alicia exclaimed.

"How do you know, Mom?" Carmen asked.

"Because I've got a daughter who's going to turn fifteen in the fall," Sophia said. "I like to do my research."

Carmen looked concerned. "We don't have that kind of money."

"Don't worry about it, *niña*," Sophia said. "We'll cross that bridge when we get there. Besides, not every *quince* costs ten thousand dollars. You can have a perfectly nice party on five thousand dollars or even less."

Alicia was starting to think that she should've just stuck to the City Hall internship. At least there, none of the budget problems were her concern! "Perfectly nice isn't going to cut it," she said. "This is the Amigas' first *quinceañera*. It's our showcase. We've got to bring the hotness or other girls won't want us to plan their event."

"Well, sometimes, having less money can make you *more*

creative," said Sophia. "Look at Carmen and the outfits that she makes. People stop her on the street because they can tell her work is couture quality. The key to working on a budget is planning and negotiating. You've got to check and recheck your budget on a daily basis, and you've got to be willing to negotiate. If a vendor wants to sell you something for a hundred dollars, try to get it for fifty. And if someone offers you something for fifty dollars, see if there's a way that you can get it for free."

"Well, we're all working for free on this one, so that's got to save money," Carmen said.

Alicia opened to a fresh page in her notebook and wrote:

Sarita's Budget
Dress: $0

"Well, the dress isn't zero dollars, because Carmen has to buy the material and sewing supplies," Sophia said.

"Good point," Alicia said. "How much, Carmen? You already did the church dress—we'll pay you back, of course."

"Sounds good. I want to use silver tulle, diamond sequins, and a satin tulle underlay for her party dress. That's not cheap," she said. "But it's a minidress, not a long, flowing gown, so we'll use less fabric. I'd say a hundred and fifty dollars. Plus extra for the church dress."

"Okay," Alicia said. "We also need to get her a white lab coat and horn-rimmed glasses for the opening dance number. That's probably another forty dollars."

"Maybe the thing to do is to make a list of everything you need and plug in the numbers later," Sophia said. "Carmen, you spend so much money at Malena's Fabric Shop, why don't you go in, explain what you are doing, and see if they'll cut you a deal?"

Suddenly an idea popped into Alicia's head. "Hey, at C. G. High's graduation performance, Mr. Jamison gets people to donate all kinds of things by promising them free advertising in the program," she said. "Maybe we can promise the vendors advertising in Sarita's program."

Sophia smiled. "That's a great idea. Do you know how many guests Sarita is planning on inviting? The more people are there, the better deals you're liable to land."

Alicia groaned. Why hadn't she gotten an exact number before? "I'll be right back," she said with a sigh.

She got up and went to call Sarita. Afterward, she came back to the table and reported, "She's having two hundred people. She says she's got a big family."

Sophia thought about it for a second. "Two hundred is a lot of people. You're bound to get some deals from people who want free advertising, but then that's also two hundred people you've got to feed."

"Feed?" Alicia asked.

"Feed," Sophia repeated. "Have you ever been to a *quince* without food?"

Alicia shook her head.

"Maribelle!" Carmen exclaimed. "Maribelle can make the food."

Alicia grinned. "*That* is a genius idea."

"You've still got to pay her for her time and buy all the groceries," Sophia reminded them.

Alicia laid her head down on the table. "I'm in so much trouble," she said.

"No," Sophia said gently. "You're just starting a business. And if it's successful, think about how impressed colleges are going to be with your accomplishment."

"Think about how much money we'll make," Carmen added.

"You might make some money, yes," Sophia said.

"But first we need that final checklist," Alicia said.

For the next two hours the girls sat and brainstormed. Finally they had their complete list of what needed money.

<u>Sarita's Budget</u>
Dress:
Shoes (Flats and heels):
Hair and makeup:

Venue:
Set design:
Ceremony fees:
Flowers and decorations:
Food and beverages:
Cake:
Music:
Photography:
Invitations:
Limo:
Favors:

Alicia and Carmen looked at each other.

"We've got a lot of work to do," Carmen pointed out.

"But at least we have a better plan now. Thank you, Sophia."

"My pleasure. But remember, you've got to plan your work and work your plan," said Sophia. "Now I've got to go pick up the girls from swim practice. See you later."

The girls were—once again—on their own.

CHAPTER 9

THE LIST FINALIZED, Carmen and Alicia took a break and went up to the bedroom Carmen shared with Una. It was about half the size of Alicia's room at home. Even though the sisters were way too old for them, the bunk beds of their childhood were still up, doing their space-saving job. The walls were a soft coral, like the color of fresh-squeezed papaya juice, and there were no taped-up posters of cute boys on the walls. Instead, Una, who hoped to go to art school, had carefully framed her best pieces—portraits of women from the barrio, their ears, necks, and fingers emblazoned with copious amounts of bling. Carmen had found reams of Missoni fabric on eBay—it was because the fabric had a manufacturing defect, but that was not at all visible to the average person—and made curtains and matching bedspreads out of the wavy knit with its lines of hot pink, yellow, and chocolate brown.

"I love your room," Alicia said, flopping down at the little vanity table that also served as Carmen and Una's desk.

Carmen's sewing machine, where she spent most of her free time, was wedged into a nook near the window so she could sew and enjoy the view of the canals at the same time.

"*Ay*, no," Carmen said, waving her hand dismissively. "We're like the old lady and the shoe up in this piece. Now, *your* room and *your* house, that's the hotness."

"Speaking of hotness—we're going to see Gaz's friend Hector spin at a club in Surfside tonight," Alicia said. "You should come."

Carmen knew what Alicia was doing. She wanted to set her up because Alicia wouldn't admit—even though they all knew it—that she liked Gaz. "Why don't I flat-iron your hair? It always looks so pretty that way," Carmen said, dodging the question.

Alicia didn't need much prodding. Her hair was naturally curly. She almost never wore it straight, because she couldn't be bothered. But on rare occasions, she did straighten it, and it always got lots of compliments. As the flatiron heated up, Carmen brushed Alicia's hair. Alicia wondered if this were what life with a sister was like—brushing each other's hair, borrowing each other's clothes. As much as Carmen complained about Una, it seemed as if having a sister could be fun.

"Come with us tonight," Alicia said. Then she cried, "Ouch!" She had forgotten to sit still and had gotten a little sting from the hot iron as it touched her scalp.

"And horn in on your date with Gaz?" Carmen asked. "No gracias, Mami."

Alicia tried to reel in the big grin that spread across her face at the words *date with Gaz*. She laughed nonetheless, then felt the laugh catch in her throat. She took a deep breath.

"It's *not* a date," she said. "So, come with me, please? Because, let's just say that I *did* like Gaz, and let's just say that he *doesn't* like me back; I'm going to need a friend to pick me up from the crying puddle I'll be if he disses me."

Carmen guffawed, and Alicia smiled. She loved the fact that, while her friend looked like America's Next Top Model, she laughed like a character from *The Simpsons*.

"Well, when you put it that way, I guess I have no choice. I can't abandon my girl in her time of need."

"Excellent!" Alicia said.

Carmen grinned. "So, you admit it? You *do* have real feelings for our dear Gaz. Is tonight the night that you tell him how you feel?"

"Maybe," Alicia said, her heart beating wildly. It felt nice to say it out loud. But why didn't Gaz do the guy thing and just ask her out on a real date? If she was the one who said something . . . and he didn't feel the same way, she'd be heartbroken. Not to mention the fact that it would also be really, *really* awkward.

Carmen ran a few more strands of hair under the flatiron. Alicia reached up and ran her fingers through her hair. She was proud of her curls, but she realized the value of changing things up. Her hair felt like silk threads in her hand.

"Thanks, C.," she said. "I love it!"

"Of course you do," Carmen said, proudly. "It's got swagger."

Alicia jumped out of the chair. "Next issue. What are you going to wear tonight?" she asked excitedly. "We've got to roll into that club with . . ."

"Swagger," Carmen said, finishing Alicia's thought and making her laugh.

Both girls were wearing T-shirts, big beaded necklaces, and skinny jeans, tucked into worn boots. But for a night out, they definitely had to take it up a notch.

"Seeing as your closet is as big as my entire bedroom," Carmen said, "I think I'm going to borrow something from you."

Alicia smiled. Maybe she shouldn't be jealous of Carmen's having a sister. Borrowing clothes, hooking up each other's hair, there were definitely days when she felt as though she and Carmen were *casi hermanas*. Not quite sisters, but close enough.

Riding in Gaz's hooptie later that night, Alicia rolled down the window and soaked in the night air.

"Notice anything different about me?" she asked Gaz playfully.

"Nope," he said.

He was staring straight ahead, ever the careful driver. She knew that no matter how many times he was offered a beer that night, he wouldn't take it. He wasn't a prude, and he never commented on what other people did. But he was the most responsible person that Alicia knew. If he said he would call at seven thirty, the phone would ring at seven twenty-nine. Alicia's mother liked to say that Gaz was "right as rain."

Alicia swung her straight hair around. "Really, nothing?"

"Not a thing."

Carmen was sitting in the back seat, so they didn't see her roll her eyes. She sometimes got a little tired of being the third wheel around Gaz and Alicia's unspoken romance. "She straightened her hair," Carmen said, in a voice that she could only hope conveyed how bored she was with the whole thing.

Gaz feigned surprise. "You straightened your hair?"

Alicia beamed. "I certainly did."

He reached over and touched it. "It's pretty."

"Get a room," Carmen mumbled.

Alicia and Gaz stole a quick glance at each other and smiled. Alicia flushed. He had to like her. No, he liked her. He really liked her. Then, because suddenly she felt completely and utterly freaked out, she said, "My brother says there are alligators in this bay. I can't believe it, but I've lived in Miami my entire life and have only ever seen a gator in the zoo." She knew it was a silly thing to say, but it was safer territory.

"Jamie says that she saw a baby gator in her cousin's toilet in the Bronx," Carmen piped up.

"And you believe her?" Gaz asked, laughing.

Carmen shrugged. "Well, I don't *not* believe her," she said, which made both Gaz and Alicia laugh.

Pura Vida, the nightclub where Gaz's friend was spinning, was like something out of a south-of-the-border brochure: bamboo walls, palm-leaf roof, and dirt floors screamed, *Puerto Rico!* and *Tulum!* The casual, palapa-style architecture seemed directly contradictory to the velvet rope that had been erected and the long line of well-dressed men and women waiting impatiently to get in.

Gaz seemed nervous. "I didn't realize it was such a scene. You'd think Hector would've given me a heads-up."

He pulled his car into the lot next to the club. A guy who looked as if he could've been on a SWAT team: clean shaven, with baseball cap, big muscles, and a windbreaker that said, *Pura Vida*, motioned for him to roll his window down. "That'll be twenty bucks," he said.

Gaz was visibly distressed, though Alicia could see he

was trying to keep his cool. Of their whole crew, he was the one with the least money, and twenty bucks for parking was a huge stretch for him.

"But we're on the list, man," Gaz said. "We're with Hector."

The parking guy shrugged. "Don't know Hector, and there's no list out here. Twenty bones, please."

Alicia reached for her purse. "I got it."

Gaz put his hand over hers and shook his head. Her hand tingled, and she wasn't sure if it was because she was worried that she might have offended him or because his hand felt so nice on hers.

"I'm good," Gaz said, passing the attendant a crisp bill.

"You know what that was," Alicia said, as they got out of the car.

"Highway robbery?" Gaz asked.

"Nope. Swagger tax," Alicia said. "We've got so much that they're taxing us on it."

Even on the short walk from the lot to the front door, they could feel the Miami heat, charging them like an offensive linebacker.

Alicia was wearing a strapless black Zoe jumpsuit with vintage Sigerson Morrison pumps. She reached up instinctively to smooth her hair.

Carmen noticed and smiled. "You're good," she reassured her. "Plus, I brought backup."

Carmen was wearing a crocheted dress by Stella McCartney that Alicia had found at a Miami consignment shop. It was a delicate dress, which was why it looked odd with the huge orange and navy tote bag with rope handles that Carmen was carrying—until, opening her purse, she revealed the flatiron.

Alicia guffawed. "No wonder you're carrying such a huge bag!"

"You know what I always say," Carmen said, grinning. "Talk softly and carry a giant purse. Of course, with the whole *Lost* theme they've got going on here, it's entirely possible that the bathrooms won't have electrical outlets. But I stand by the big-purse thing."

Inside the club, they quickly found Hector, who was dressed to the nines in a Benjamin Bixby straw hat, a purple and white pinstriped shirt, and khaki linen pants. Carmen was quick to point out how good he looked. Alicia noticed, but it just gave her a sweeter appreciation for Gaz's Gap polo and chinos.

Besides, she thought, It'll be a cold day in the Keys before I date a guy who dresses better than me!

The DJ was playing a trippy MIA-Shakira mash-up: "Sunshowers" mixed with "Te Vuelvas." But the crowd was loving it, and the hundred or so people on the dance floor didn't seem to mind that there wasn't as much as a ceiling fan in the place.

Alicia looked over at Carmen. "It's so-o-o-o hot."

Carmen nodded.

Both of the girls were sweating, despite discreet attempts to wipe their faces with the napkins on the table.

"Dancing will only make us hotter," Alicia observed.

"It will," Carmen answered.

"Do we care?"

"Not really."

Laughing, the two girls jumped up and joined the crowd, full of swiveling hips and moving feet. Alicia sang along to the chorus, the Spanish words feeling sweet on her tongue, like chocolate-covered churros.

When they finally took a break from dancing, Hector ordered a round of virgin mojitos. When they had quenched their thirst, Hector invited Carmen to hang out with him in the DJ booth during his set. Despite her earlier worries about Alicia's matchmaking, Carmen beamed. Alicia watched her friend stride across the dance floor.

"Take care of my *amiga-hermana*," she called out to Hector.

"Or else," she muttered to herself.

"Hey, I think I left my cell in the car," Gaz said when they'd been alone for a few minutes. "Come with me?"

Alicia shrugged. Gaz was always leaving his cell phone somewhere. She'd once seen him walk into her house, open the freezer door, pull out a pint of ice cream, and, after serving himself a couple of scoops, put his cell in the freezer while the ice cream sat on the counter, melting.

She followed him out the door of the club. As they approached the parking lot, he suddenly stopped.

"This is good," he said, looking not at her, but at the canopy of stars above them.

Alicia was confused. "Good for what? I thought you needed your cell."

"Nah. It's just too hot inside. Will you dance with me?" he asked. He reached out to her, and Alicia thought she would die. Her heart was pounding wildly; she hoped beyond hope that her underarm deodorant lived up to expectations, because she was sweating in a decidedly not delicate way.

Alicia shook her head. Was this really—finally—happening? "But we can't even hear the music out here."

Gaz said, "I'm going to sing for you."

He held her in his arms and began to sing a song he had written about waves and hellos—*olas* and *holas*.

Alicia pressed her head against his chest, surprised at how natural it felt. She wondered if he would kiss her and if he would be able to tell that, apart from a very wretched game of Seven Minutes in Heaven back in the sixth grade, she had never really *kiss*-kissed a boy before.

She felt him pull away from her, and she closed her eyes, parting her lips ever so slightly. She waited. And waited.

Finally, opening her eyes, she noticed that he was looking not at her, but up at the stars. Her heart sank.

"We should go back inside before they miss us," he said, looking back at her.

"Absolutely," she replied, willing her pulse to stop racing and her sweat glands to stop working overtime.

Then Gaz did the awful thing that cemented the horrible moment and set Alicia's cheeks blazing—and not in a good way. He kissed her on the forehead and began to walk back to the club.

Alicia did not know much about boys and dating, but one thing she did know was that boys who wanted to be your boyfriend did *not* kiss you on the forehead. Did they?

Back inside, Gaz and Alicia sat across the table from each other, looking everywhere but into each other's eyes. In the DJ booth, Hector was playing Daddy Yankee, but Alicia didn't have the desire to shake her groove thing anymore. She sat across from Gaz, sipping her mojito and wondering why he hadn't kissed her.

Forty-five minutes later, Hector's set was done. Alicia and Gaz still sat across from each other. But somehow, during the set, their hands had stretched across the table, and now their fingers were touching at the very tips. It wasn't exactly holding hands, but Alicia almost liked it more. It was as if there were little crackles of electricity where their hands met. It made up for the forehead kiss—mostly.

Arriving back at their table, Carmen looked at her friend and raised an eyebrow. Alicia looked right back and thought, *Chica*, if you only knew; touching Gaz's hand is the least of it. But as confusing as it all was, she didn't want to talk about it with Carmen. She wanted to hold on tight to the sweet memory of Gaz dancing with her. Alicia feared, somewhat irrationally, she knew, that if she told Carmen about *every-thing* that had happened, it would seem a little too real. And maybe Alicia would have to confront the fact that while he was very fond of her, Gaz just didn't like her in the same way she liked him.

CHAPTER 10

EVEN THOUGH Alicia would have been content to dwell on Gaz and his mixed messages, she had a *quince-añera* to plan. And the closer they got to Sarita's *quince*, the more stressed—and difficult—Alicia got. With two weeks left till the big day, she began to focus *only* on the *quince*. For her internship, she was supposed to be working on a liaison request for a *telenovela* production company for the Office of Film and Cultural Affairs, but she spent most of her mornings keeping tabs on her crew.

One morning, during a city council meeting, she ducked into her father's office to make a few calls out from under Lori's watchful eye.

Alicia sat down at her father's desk, dialed nine for an outside line, and called Gaz.

"What are you doing?" she asked when he picked up. She spoke to the members of the club so often that she didn't even bother to say hello. Still, when it was Gaz, she was often flustered.

"At this very second, I'm folding a new shipment of lightweight cashmere sweaters," Gaz said. "I'm at work."

"Have you and your brothers worked on the mariachi number for Sarita's father-daughter *vals*?" she asked.

"I told you we did," Gaz said. It was only eleven in the morning, but it was the third time that day that Alicia had called him. He had a good mind to start ignoring her phone calls, but he retained the hope—a hope that was fading fast—that the next time she called, she'd be back to her old self, saying, "Hey, *loco*, what's the *qué pasa?*"

"The *vals* is very important, and the mariachi music is Sarita's big cultural nod to her family; you've got to get it right," Alicia said.

Gaz had volunteered to learn Sarita's father's favorite song and to play it with his brothers. "We've never done mariachi before," he had told Sarita, "but I think we could make it both fresh and old-school."

"That's exactly what I want for my *vals*," Sarita had said, beaming.

Alicia knew that Gaz needed to show off his band's stuff if Sarita were going to get "exactly" what she wanted. It was, she told herself, the reason she kept calling, and it had nothing to do with hearing his smooth, sweet voice. Nothing at all.

After checking on Gaz, Alicia called Carmen. *"Dígame,"* she asked. "How's that dress coming?"

"The same way it was when you asked me two hours ago—fine." Carmen said. "Stop sweating me!"

"I'm just making sure we're all on target," Alicia said. "We've got a lot to do over the next few weeks. And it's my job to make sure that it all gets done."

Carmen sighed. "It'll all get done *a lot* faster if you don't call me every five minutes."

She was about to blow a gasket, but Alicia was oblivious.

"Okay," she said. "Sounds good. Just text me this afternoon with an update."

"Good-bye," Carmen said.

"Don't forget, we're meeting tomorrow afternoon at three," Alicia said. But it seemed that Carmen had already hung up. She dialed her friend's number again.

"Hey," Alicia said "I think you hung up."

"I said, 'good-bye,'" Carmen grumbled.

"I just wanted to remind you that we have a meeting tomorrow at Lario's, at three."

"Good-bye, Alicia," Carmen said, hanging up the phone again.

Alicia thought it was interesting how planning Sarita's *quince* was really bringing out people's true colors. Carmen lived in a house of total chaos. You would think she would have been able to handle a little pressure. But she was clearly flipping out. Alicia grabbed her iPhone and made a note to give everybody a pep talk about staying organized and *calm* at the meeting.

She put an "urgent" flag on the pep-talk note and then called Jamie, who answered the phone screaming.

"Stop calling me!" Jamie yelled. "You are working my last nerves."

Once again, Alicia failed to recognize that the stress her friends were exhibiting had anything to do with her.

"Look," Alicia said. "I know what you're going through. We are working our butts off. We're not getting paid, and Sarita's *quince* is two weeks away. That's why we've got to keep our cool, help each other out, and try to remember that we got into this business to have fun."

"Do you want to help me out?" Jamie asked.

"Of course," Alicia said. "That's why I called."

"Then stop calling me!" Jamie said, and she hung up.

Alicia sent Jamie a text message: *Hola. I think we had a bad connection. What's going on with the plan for Sarita's hair, makeup? How many rsvp's has she gotten? Have you ordered the favors? I'd like an update soon.*

Alicia looked at her watch. It was only a little after eleven. She retyped the last line: *I'd like an update by noon. Ciao.*

The next day, Sarita, Alicia, and Jamie headed to Paso Doble boutique to shop for *quince* heels. These were one of the few items that Amigas Inc. couldn't actually make. Shoes were, of course, a big deal. At the church, before the big party, the father helps the girl having the *quince* change from flats into high heels, to symbolize her transition into womanhood. Sarita had already chosen a pair of silver ballet flats to wear to the church. Now she needed something fierce, her first pair of real heels, to wear to the party.

Everything else was coming together brilliantly. Sarita loved the idea of re-creating a little bit of Cape Canaveral on South Beach, and Alex was completely psyched to build them a model rocket and the rest of the space-age set. Carmen was going to start final fittings for the dresses on Wednesday. Little by little, the *quince* was coming together.

The shoe store had been open for twenty minutes by the time the girls made their way inside. On this particular shopping trip, Alicia and Jamie were the designated grown-ups, with the responsibility for an envelope full of cash from Sarita's mother. But they soon found themselves falling into girlfriend mode as Sarita tried on shoe after gorgeous shoe.

Although it was lovely, they rejected a white d'Orsay pump as being too formal for the beach setting and Cape Canaveral theme.

A pair of white T-straps would have been, as Jamie put it, "supercute with a white T-shirt and a pair of dark-dyed jeans. But too informal for a *quince*."

Jamie and Sarita fell hard for a pair of hot pink stilettos, but Alicia rejected them as too high to dance in.

"Do I have to dance? Can't I just stand around looking gorgeous?" Sarita joked, teetering around the store like a ballerina wearing pointe shoes for the very first time.

"Of course you have to dance," Alicia said. "You have the first *vals* with your dad. You have the group dance with the *chambelanes* and *damas*. Plus your opening solo. But don't you worry. I'll teach you everything you need to know."

Sarita did three more tiny-stepping tours (wobbling the whole way) around the shoe-store floor before sitting down and taking the heels off. "Speaking of dancing, I've picked my escort for the evening. His name is Diego," she said, beaming. "I've only known him for a few weeks. He lives on the second floor of my building. Seeing him in the elevator is, like, the highlight of my day. So I just decided to ask him to be my *chambelán*, and he said yes." Sarita had moved on to a pair of silver sandals with two braided straps across the insteps. "What do you think?" she asked Alicia.

Jamie had gone off to negotiate with the store's owner for a discount, in exchange for an ad in Sarita's *quince* program.

"Do you like this one?" Sarita held out her foot so that Alicia could get a closer look at the shoe.

Alicia raised an eyebrow.

"No client of the Amigas is turning fifteen in half-inch kitten heels," Alicia said decisively.

"Shoes are what I do, I'm the image consultant, and I say they look great," Jamie said, coming back in time to overhear Alicia.

Sarita and Jamie exchanged glances, uncertain as to whether Alicia was ignoring them or just hadn't heard them. She'd wandered off to the high-end section of the store.

She returned with a pair of black-patent-leather Yves Saint Laurent cage booties.

"You've got to be kidding me," Sarita said.

"Try them on," Alicia insisted. "They're your size."

"They may be my size, but they're definitely not my style," Sarita said.

Alicia looked slightly annoyed. "You're a Miami girl now. Styles change, *chica*."

Jamie grabbed Alicia by the shoulder. "May I talk to you for a sec?" she asked through clenched teeth. She didn't wait for an answer, but simply dragged Alicia to a quiet corner of the store.

"Alicia, come on," she said. "I'm all for speaking your mind, you know; I do it all the time. But you're way out of line here. This is Sarita's *quince*, not yours."

"Don't you think I know that?" Alicia said, huffily. "But her party is *our* calling card. It's got to be over the top or else we've got no business."

"Well, you'd better check yourself before you wreck yourself," Jamie said, throwing her hands up in the air.

When they rejoined her, Sarita was standing in the designer heels, her hands pressed against the store's full-length mirror. It quickly became apparent that she was holding on for balance, and for dear life.

"I get that these shoes are fierce, fabulous, and flawless," she said, "but if I can't walk in them, then it's going to be a pretty miserable *quince*."

Alicia shrugged her shoulders and replied, in a world-weary tone that implied that she was years and not merely months older than Sarita, "We've all got to suffer for beauty." Then she handed her credit card to the salesperson and said, "She'll take them. My treat."

It was the first time that Alicia had used the card outside of Barnes & Noble, and she half expected the charge to be declined, as if her parents could see that she was spending hundreds of dollars on designer shoes for Sarita's *quince*.

Sarita looked both embarrassed and uncomfortable, "These are really expensive shoes, Alicia. I can't let you spend so much money on me."

Alicia signed the credit-card receipt with a flourish. "It's a done deal. Consider it my *quince* present to you."

"I consider it the beginning of Queen Alicia's reign," Jamie muttered under her breath.

CHAPTER 11

ALICIA KNEW that it was probably not the brightest idea to schedule a dance rehearsal in the wedding room at City Hall. But give a *chica* a break, she thought. It was Thursday, and Sarita's *quince* was less than two weeks away. Sarita might have been a rocket scientist, but she could barely walk, much less dance, in high heels. Not to mention the fact that her *chambelán*, Diego, was clearly the guy born to defy the wisdom of Gloria Estefan. While it may have been true that the rhythm was going to get 99.9 percent of the Greater Miami population, Diego belonged to the .1 percent that the rhythm was *always* going to miss. After running him through some simple steps a day earlier, Alicia had simplified the choreography. Then she'd simplified it again. But still, Sarita was teetering in her heels and Diego was tripping over his two left feet. Alicia scheduled the dance rehearsal at City Hall, because she was not going to have a goofy number ruin the first event run by the Amigas. Not on her watch. It was time to practice.

She had checked the schedule to make sure no weddings were planned for that morning. She had also made sure, before scheduling a thirty-minute dance rehearsal, that Lori would be out of the office at her anger management course, where she always went at eleven on Thursday mornings. It made perfect sense to rehearse at City Hall, because Alicia and Sarita were already there, which meant they could eliminate the pesky business of arranging a ride or taking a bus after work. It was a foolproof plan.

Or so she thought.

Approximately fifteen minutes into the rehearsal, the mayor walked in with the number one tennis star in Miami, who had decided to elope with her longtime boyfriend. It turned out that Lori had purposely not put it on the schedule so as not to alert the press. Alicia was right in the middle of trying to teach Sarita and Diego the sexy *paso doble* from Shakira's "La Tortura" video. To demonstrate the singer's sexy belly dance, Alicia had knotted her blouse below the bra (and done the same to Sarita's).

To make matters worse, her father had joined the wedding party to serve as an official witness. It was clear from the flash of his dark eyes and the furrow of his brow that he was not, in any way, amused. But the real drama had yet to unfold. Lori's anger management class had been canceled and she followed behind the mayor, the tennis star, the tennis star's intended, and the deputy mayor.

When Lori saw Alicia, her face turned scarlet. If Alicia hadn't been so nervous, she would have commented that a little blusher would have done wonders for Lori. But then the supervisor started fuming. "I should have known," Lori said icily. "This is completely unacceptable. Please leave—you're fired!"

Alicia jumped to turn off the music, which was booming from her laptop, then ran to cower behind her father. Her *papi* would protect her. "Dad, I didn't want to tell you, but I'm pretty sure Lori is nuts," she whispered.

Mr. Cruz seemed less interested in Lori's histrionics—she'd moved on from the subject of Alicia and was now screaming about the jerk who'd cut her off in traffic that morning on I-95—and more interested in his daughter's misbehavior.

"You are fifteen years old," Mr. Cruz said. "Show some humility, *hija*! I did not arrange this internship so you could party in City Hall with your friends!"

"We're not partying," Alicia protested. "We're rehearsing for Sarita's *quince*!"

"Leave me out of it, *niña*," Sarita said.

Turning back to Alicia, Mr. Cruz said, "Lori is right. This is unacceptable. You are *not* here to bare your midriff. You are *not* here to blare loud music in a government building. You *are* here to listen and learn. You haven't done much of either since you showed up for this internship, according to

Lori's reports. I will not let you waste an opportunity another student would give her eyeteeth for. I agree with Lori—go home."

With that, he turned and walked away.

Alicia couldn't believe it. Her own *papi*, giving her the boot. Her mother was going to *kill* her. She was never going to Harvard, and her parents were going to rub it in her face for the rest of her natural-born life. Her father, who was always the mellow one, was being such a hothead!

If he had seen Sarita and Diego dance, he would have understood why she had to schedule extra rehearsals by any means necessary. It wasn't her fault that the wedding hall was being used for a top secret celebrity wedding. She'd checked the schedule. As they said in the legal profession, she'd done her due diligence. She was *on time* every morning. This was largely because her dad gave her a ride. But still, *fíjase*, it took an effort to get up early, be dressed and ready on time. Her father was tripping. Totally taking his problems out on her. He was up for election the following year. It was only his first term as deputy mayor. Maybe he was worried about losing his appointment. That had to be it. He was *so* in love with public office that having a Latina daughter who was trying to do something for her *hermanas* did not fit his image of the campaign-friendly daughter. He hated her. Why else, how else, could he fire her, just like that?

She went to her desk and packed up her things, mostly stuff related to Sarita's *quince*: CDs, fabric swatches, photographers' portfolios, and she piled them all into the shopping bags Lori kept in the cabinet in the coffee room. It didn't take her long. The buildings at City Hall were always cold, so even when it was a hundred degrees outside, Alicia kept a black cardigan at her desk. She picked up the cardigan and the black Coach tote that her mother had gotten her as a gift to celebrate the new job. There were some papers on her desk, but she figured that Lori would figure out what went where. It wasn't her problem anymore. She'd been canned.

Walking through the security scanner at the front door, she willed herself not to cry.

"Checking out early?" Mr. Bennett, one of the security guards, asked. He was an older African American man, and he always had a kind word for everyone, even Lori.

"Something like that," Alicia replied.

Walking out of the building, she felt the heat descend on her. She walked down the street to the bus stop, dragging her feet; she *hated* taking the bus, but since he'd just basically fired her, she was fairly confident that her father wasn't going to drive her home. Or speak to her—ever again.

Alicia looked at her watch; it was almost two o'clock. She'd been out for a few hours already and was bored, with a capital *B*. Wow, she thought sarcastically, time flies when you're unemployed. Luckily, Sarita and Jamie were coming over at three to try out hairstyles. That gave her something to do. She went to the bathroom to give herself a pep talk in the mirror. Despite the fact that she loved fashion, Alicia was a five-minutes-in-the-mirror-makeup girl. Standing in the bathroom with no internship to rush off to, she took a deep breath and tried to let it all sink in. Then she began talking to herself out loud: "Look, you were fired from an internship you really liked. You were yelled at by your dad, who, up until recently, you were pretty sure respected you as a smart, up-and-coming Latina on her way. You can't change the past, but you can concentrate on the present. Sarita's *quince* is around the corner, and if it's perfect, no one's going to remember the big blank spot on your college résumé where the City Hall internship was supposed to go. So, gather the troops, and get ready to kick butt, because you've got a party to plan!"

Alicia stopped just short of high-fiving herself in the mirror and shrugged.

She took off her work shoes, a pair of slightly scuffed Dior heels that were a hand-me-down from her mom, and tossed them across the room. She wouldn't be needing those anymore.

And since she had a little time to spare before the great

quince hair project began, she decided to check in on her crew.

She called Jamie first.

"Hey, Jamie, what's up?" she asked.

"What's up is that I'm on a bus, on my way to your house," Jamie said, exasperated. "If you call me one more time, I swear, I will turn around and go home."

"No problem," Alicia said. "So what's your ETA?"

"I'm losing you," Jamie said, crumbling a ball of paper into the phone. Then she grumbled, "I'm trying *really* hard to lose you."

Alicia, however, didn't hear her. She had hung up and was already calling Gaz.

"Gaz: the mariachi number. I need to know your band can deliver," Alicia said.

"Alicia," Gaz said. "You are bugging out. What is going on with you?"

"Nothing," Alicia said. "Just got to hold it all together."

"It's together, Lici," Gaz said. "This is so not like you. Do you want to talk? I can come over after work. My shift ends at seven."

"I'm cool," Alicia lied. "Just taking care of business." She and Gaz hadn't been alone since the club. They hadn't even *talked* about what had happened. Would it be weird?

"Business will take care of itself, *Mamita*," Gaz said,

interrupting her thoughts. "Who's going to take care of you?"

Mamita? Wait, *was* Gaz her boyfriend now? It would be so nice if something in her life turned out the way she'd hoped. She wanted to tell him everything, about losing her internship, about being so scared that something might go wrong with Sarita's *quince* that she couldn't even think straight. She wanted to tell him that she liked him. But she had just been fired, and she was feeling like a big, giant loser. And if at this very second he liked her, the minute he found out the truth he was bound to stop. She crumpled up a piece of paper right into the earpiece of her cell.

"Sorry, Gaz," she said. "I'm losing you." Then she hung up the phone. She would deal with that all later. She hoped.

When Jamie rang the doorbell, Alicia had pushed thoughts of Gaz out of her head and was ready with a whole new plan for Sarita's hair.

"Hey, come in," she said. "Look at these pictures I've printed out. I was thinking that Sarita needs a more grown-up look. She needs something modern and cool, to fit the space theme. She needs . . ."

Jamie held up a hand. "Back it up, *chica*. I thought hair was *my* domain."

"It is, it is," Alicia said. "I just totally think it should look like this."

"Natalie Portman in *V for Vendetta*?" Jamie said, holding up a picture Alicia had printed out. "Don't you think that's a little harsh?"

"We've got to make Sarita's *quince* fashion-forward," Alicia insisted.

Jamie rolled her eyes. "And you don't think *I* know what fashion-forward is?"

It was a totally ridiculous question, because Jamie was always one step ahead of the fashion curve, as evidenced by the outfit she was wearing that day: a charcoal gray T-shirt that she'd pimped out with chiffon ruffles on the sleeves, stove-pipe jeans, red gladiator sandals, and bright yellow nail polish.

"So, are you going to do the cut or not?" Alicia asked, putting a hand on her hip.

"Are you going to stay in your lane and let me do what I want?" Jamie asked.

"Nope," Alicia said.

"Then, nope," Jamie said, handing Alicia back the picture of Natalie Portman's bald head. "I'm outta here, *chica*."

Turning on the heel of her gladiator sandal, Jamie walked down Alicia's driveway without saying another word.

Alicia couldn't believe it. Jamie was straight tripping! A *quince* was a massive production, like a show or a movie. It needed a director, and Alicia was the natural choice. *She* was the one who had formed Amigas. *She* was the one who had brought them all together. If Sarita's party did not wind up the most unique, memorable, *quince* that Miami had ever seen, then everyone would blame only one person—her.

CHAPTER 12

ALICIA WENT back into the house, determined to see her vision through. She didn't need Jamie's diva antics anyway. She would just do Sarita's hair and makeup.

A few minutes later, Sarita arrived. She looked super-adorable in a white tank, a long blue and gray boyfriend cardigan, and denim shorts.

"Hey!" Alicia gave her an *abrazo*.

"Sorry, I'm a few minutes late," Sarita apologized. "The bus took forever!"

"Don't even worry about it," Alicia said. "Come on in."

"Tough break about you being fired like that," Sarita said.

"I'm not worried," Alicia said. "Now I can give your *quinceañera* my full attention."

"But I thought the internship was the cornerstone of your master plan to get into Harvard and conquer the world."

Alicia cringed. That *had* been the plan. But things had changed. She was only a sophomore. If she built Amigas Inc.

into the top *quince* planning business in southern Florida, not only would Harvard have to bow down, but she would be able to pay her own tuition. She smiled for a moment, imagining the scene: her senior year; the day they'd all been waiting for. The big fat envelope from Harvard would arrive. It would say—to paraphrase—*Congratulations, Alicia Cruz, you are the bomb. We'd be honored to have a fab Latina sister like you attend our school. In fact, we'd like to do something unprecedented and enroll all of the founding members of Amigas Incorporated.*

Alicia smiled, lost in the fantasy. Her mother would faint, of course. Her father would apologize for firing her from her very first internship. Then, after her prom and her graduation, Alicia's parents would drive her to Cambridge—a long road trip from Miami, but her parents would need the time to tell her how much they'd underestimated her. When she arrived at Harvard, after she'd gotten unpacked at her dorm, said hello to her roommate, and gone to the business office to settle that year's tuition, her parents would take out their checkbook. But Alicia, the most successful teen entrepreneur that South Beach had ever seen, would say, "No worries, Mom and Dad, I've got this." And she would pay her own tuition, because Amigas Inc. would be such a radically successful business. And it all started way back when, with Sarita's *quince* and an unfortunate incident that they'd all have preferred to forget.

Alicia didn't realize she'd been standing in the hallway, staring at the David Siqueiros lithograph hanging on the wall, until . . .

"Are you okay, *niña*?" Sarita asked. "It's been a rough day; I get it. I can come back tomorrow."

Alicia smiled, trying now to fake the confidence that had been stripped away from her along with her internship. "No way, I'm cool," she said.

They walked into the kitchen, where Maribelle was preparing dinner.

"Are you two hungry?" Maribelle asked.

"I'm good," Alicia said.

"Me, too," said Sarita.

Maribelle raised an eyebrow. "Don't get too skinny. Men don't like it. Real *chicas* have curves!"

Alicia smiled. "We know, we know." She turned to Sarita and asked, "Do you want some of Maribelle's famous cucumber lemonade?"

"*Agua de pepino?*" Sarita asked.

Maribelle beamed. There were few things she loved more than teenagers who knew their *cultura*.

"*Ay, qué bueno,*" Maribelle said. "*Tú lo conoces?*"

"*Claro!*" Sarita answered. "*Mi abuela lo hacen todo el tiempo en Loreto.*"

Alicia scowled playfully. "Enough already! Come on, Sarita, let's go to my room," she said. "We've got a ton to do."

"Te veo," Sarita told Maribelle, hanging on to her lemonade as Alicia dragged her away.

"Buena suerte!" Maribelle said with a wink.

"This is, like, the coolest room ever," Sarita said, when they got upstairs. She was looking through the bay window toward the pool.

Part of Alicia's fifteenth-birthday gift was the chance to redecorate her room any way she wanted. She had gone with a black-and-white theme. The ceiling and fixtures were all a creamy alabaster white. The walls were charcoal blackboard paint, which Alicia had covered in inspirational sayings. The bedspread was a black-and-white zebra print that matched the ottoman in front of Alicia's dressing table. Two chairs, one black and one white, of course, faced the window, which overlooked the pool. Alicia had to admit it was pretty fierce.

"Thanks," she said. "Why don't you sit at the dressing table and we'll get started on your hair?"

"Aren't we going to wait for Jamie?" Sarita asked, looking a little concerned.

"Um, something came up with Jamie," Alicia said nervously. "I'm going to be doing your hair."

"But I liked the style that Jamie had come up with," Sarita said. "She's even going to loan me her favorite pair of Me&Ro earrings, that she got in the East Village."

"This'll be better," Alicia said. "And you don't need to go to New York to get Me&Ro; we can order them online."

"It's just that Jamie has been so sweet to me," Sarita said.

"No te preocupes," she said. "I'm going to hook you up."

Sarita shrugged. "I guess that's okay. Your hair always looks supercute."

"Thanks," Alicia said. She was wearing her hair in a side ponytail that day, with loose curls that she'd hot-rollered earlier that morning.

"So, can I look at some pictures?" Sarita asked. "Jamie said she was going to make me a portfolio of styles to pick from."

"Well, I've got a really cool idea," Alicia said. "But I want it to be a surprise."

"If you say so," Sarita said.

Alicia put some Shakira on the CD player and faced the dressing-table chair away from the mirror. She opened a drawer and took out her teasing comb, a bag of plastic clips, and a pair of scissors.

She combed Sarita's curly hair back, then divided it into sections with clips. Holding one section up she said, "Are you ready?"

"Born ready," Sarita answered.

Alicia cut the first piece. And another. And another. She kept snipping until there was no more hair to snip in that section. Sarita, who had been idly flipping through a magazine, looked up. She looked at the cut hair on her shoulders and the ground. Grabbing a hand mirror off Alicia's dressing table, she held it up so that she could see the back of her head. And then, she screamed.

"You cut off all my hair! You cut off all my hair!"

"I told you to trust me!" Alicia cried.

"To style my hair, not destroy it!" Sarita started sobbing. She rubbed her hand over the scratchy exposed piece of scalp. "Now I've got a bald spot. My *quince* is less than two weeks away, and I'm going to look like a total freak!"

"Not if you let me finish the cut," Alicia said.

"Finish the cut? Are you *absolutamente, completamente, loca*?" Sarita cried through her tears. "This is the worst day of my life!"

She stood up and raced out of the room.

Alicia ran after her. "Don't you even want to see the inspiration photo? I was going to give you a Natalie Portman cut for your *quince*."

Sarita stopped. "Natalie Portman?"

"She's cool, right?" Alicia looked hopefully at the other girl. "Totally modern, totally classic style, right?"

Sarita was still crying, but her sobs had dwindled to a whimper.

"I'm listening," she said.

"I'll be right back with the photo."

Alicia ran back to her room and grabbed the picture.

"See?" she said, coming back. She handed the picture to Sarita. "It totally goes with your *quince* theme."

"Bald?" Sarita said. "*V for Vendetta* bald? Did you think I was going to go to my *quince* with no hair? I *love* my hair! I want to look beautiful at my party, not like some science-fiction character."

"You asked me to make you a cool *quince*," Alicia insisted. "That's all I was doing."

"That's right," Sarita said. "A cool *quince*. Not some sort of freak show. You're crazy. *Eres loca, loca, loca.*"

Sarita started crying again. "This is the worst day of my life," she repeated. Then she raced down the hallway and into the kitchen. Pausing, she turned and made herself clearer. "No, the worst day of my life was when I met you. *Loca, loca, loca.*"

Alicia shuddered as Sarita slammed the front door.

Maribelle, who had been sautéing chicken for the arroz con pollo, turned the burner down on the stove.

"What's wrong, *mi amor*?" she asked.

Alicia sat on a stool at the kitchen counter. Before she could get the words out of her mouth, she felt her eyes fill with tears. "Oh, let's see," she said. "My dad fired me from my internship. The Amigas' first client just deserted us. And, oh, yeah, all my friends hate me. All I was trying to do was help people. Sarita needed a fabulous *quince* on a budget.

Gaz wanted to work on his music. Carmen wanted to show off her designs. Jamie wanted to launch her career as a stylist. At least I *thought* they did. I *know* I wanted to start a business. I thought I could kill all of these birds with one stone. Instead, I've just ruined everything."

Maribelle rubbed Alicia's shoulders and gave her a big *abrazo*. "When everything goes wrong, there is only one thing to do."

"What's that?" Alicia said.

"Make it right," Maribelle said.

Alicia sighed. "That's easier said than done."

"Come on," Maribelle said, reaching into a kitchen drawer for pen and paper. "You're a smart girl, and I am a very smart woman. Together, we'll figure this out."

She handed the pen and purple-lined notepad to Alicia. "Let's make a list."

"I don't think it'll help," Alicia said, grumpily.

"Well, it couldn't hurt," Maribelle said. "What would you need to do to fix things?"

Alicia stared at the blank notebook page. Across the top, she wrote:

How to Fix My Life
1. Change my name.
2. Move to Alaska.

She handed the list to Maribelle. "Done," she said.

Maribelle smiled. *"No seas tonta,"* she said, handing the pad back to Alicia. "Try again. What can you do to patch things up with everybody? Take it one person at a time."

Alicia took the pen and began to write. She was silent for a very long time. Maribelle went back to her cooking, but she watched as Alicia wrote things down, tore the page out, crumpled it up, and began again. Alicia threw out page after page. She drank five glasses of cucumber lemonade. She went to the bathroom. Not once did she say a word to Maribelle. She started writing again and, a while later, looked up and said, "I think I'm done."

She handed Maribelle her list.

How to Make Things Right, by Alicia Cruz

1. Apologize to Daddy and ask him for a second chance with my internship.

2. Work very hard at City Hall. Do not make quince calls or do quince business at the job.

3. Apologize to Sarita.

4. Stop micro-managing Carmen, Jaz, and Jamie.

"This is a *very* good list," Maribelle said.

"What if it doesn't work?" Alicia asked.

"When you follow your *corazón*," Maribelle said, giving Alicia a *besito* on the forehead, "things always work out."

CHAPTER 13

THAT NIGHT, ALICIA'S parents arrived home together—and in silence. Maribelle, aware that Alicia needed all the help she could get, had scrapped that evening's dinner plan of arroz con pollo and had instead driven to Whole Foods to shop for a meal that would put Alicia's dad—and mom—in the mood for forgiveness. The chicken dish she had been preparing would keep, but that night they would dine on saffron rice, *tostones*, ripe avocado sprinkled with Hawaiian pink sea salt, and plantain-encrusted snapper. Upon hearing her parents' car in the driveway, Alicia reached into the freezer for two ice-cold glasses of Maribelle's special *mojitos*.

She waited and watched as her mother kicked off her eggplant purple Manolo mules and her father slung his suit jacket over the dining room chair. Following her parents into the family room, she handed them each a drink. They both said a quiet *gracias*, but Alicia could tell that their moods were as frosty as the *mojitos*.

"Dad, I'm so sorry," she began. "If you'll just give me a chance—"

Enrique Cruz looked at his wife. "Please tell her not to speak to me right now."

Alicia's mother sighed deeply, took a sip of her *mojito* and said, "Your father says . . ."

Alicia couldn't believe it. They were acting as immature as kids at her school. "I heard him," she said, sulkily. She walked back into the kitchen, where Maribelle was slicing an avocado into mini works of art.

"They're never going to forgive me," Alicia moaned. "No matter what I do, they're going to be mad."

Maribelle put down the knife and considered Alicia, her dark curls, her sad brown eyes, her long lashes wet with tears. She had no children of her own, but she had Alicia and Alex. Loving them, raising them, had been the best part of her job.

"You're growing up, and you have to learn how to take responsibility for doing wrong," Maribelle finally said. "'Sorry' is not always going to make things go away like *that*." She snapped her fingers.

"But you said that all I had to do is follow my heart and make things right." Alicia knew that she was whining. But she was starting to get frustrated.

"I never said it would be easy," Maribelle said.

"So, what do I do?" Alicia asked, genuinely confused.

"Stay humble, pay attention, apologize as soon as your *papi* gives you the chance," Maribelle said.

"And if that doesn't work?" Alicia said.

"It will work," Maribelle assured her. *"Ten confianza."*

Maribelle had finished her handiwork on the avocado and, as they had done a hundred times before, she and Alicia began to set the table.

"You know, I'm not entirely sure that it was a good idea for you to skip your *quinceañera*," Maribelle said.

"I didn't skip it, I just chose to to take a cool trip instead of having a corny Cinderella theme party and a big poufy dress."

"But being a *quince* is more than the party and the big dress," the older woman said. "Planning the party gives you time to consider the kind of woman you want to be and how you hope to present yourself to the world. I'm not sure you get the same experience from buying plane tickets online."

"I didn't even buy the tickets. My mom did."

"My point, exactly," Maribelle said. "When you're standing at the altar in front of your family and friends, there's no way to just read those vows without some of it sinking in."

Alicia put down the stack of plates she was holding. "Wait a second, Maribelle. Did you have a *quinceañera*?"

Maribelle put a hand on her hip and gave Alicia a saucy look. "Of course I did," she said. "You and your friends did not invent *quinceañeras*, you know."

Alicia was dumbfounded. "But you never told me that before."

"I'm a grown woman, and I've had a very full life," Maribelle said. "There are many things I haven't told you."

"Will you show me your *quince* pictures?" Alicia asked.

"Maybe," Maribelle said.

"And who was your lead *chambelán*?"

"The man who would become my first husband," Maribelle said, with a wink.

"First husband!" Alicia squealed. "I didn't know you had more than one!"

"As I said, there's a lot you don't know, *preciosa*," Maribelle said.

Alicia hugged her, grateful to have Maribelle as her substitute *abuela*, thankful that for at least a few minutes, she had managed to forget exactly how much trouble she was in and how scared she was that she might not get out of it.

Luckily, the forgiveness dinner seemed to have the desired effect. Her father spoke only to her mother and Alex through most of the meal. But Alicia could see that his shoulders were not as hunched, and the furrow in his brow was softening.

Finally, when Maribelle emerged from the kitchen with dessert, lavender crème brûlée, Alicia summoned enough confidence to take her chance.

"Dad, can I say something?" she asked.

Her father's expression was stony, but he nodded. "Fine, say something."

"I messed up big-time," Alicia said. "You gave me a really great opportunity, and I took it for granted. I became completely obsessed with Sarita's *quince* and the business, and the way that I behaved at the office didn't show how proud I am of you and being your daughter."

Both of Alicia's parents looked at her with more than a little surprise. Her mother spoke first.

"Well, Alicia," she said, "while I don't condone your behavior, I have to say, I'm very impressed with the way you are taking responsibility for your actions."

"Yeah, who's your speechwriter, Squeak?" Alex asked, using the old nickname from the time when Alicia was a baby and her first attempts at talking came out as a series of high-pitched squeaks. Hardly anyone ever called her that anymore, except for members of her extended family who hadn't seen her in years—and Alex, when he wanted to give her a hard time.

Alicia ignored her brother and tried to focus on what Maribelle had said about becoming a young woman and how you wanted to present yourself to the world. Maybe she had missed out on more than she'd realized by not having a *quince*. But she was going to be fifteen for five more months; nothing was stopping her from making every last moment of that year count.

"Dad," she said. "Is there any way you can get me another shot at that internship? If not this summer, then maybe for the fall?"

Her father paused. "Actually," he finally said, "I did not get a chance to speak to Lori today, so they haven't made your quitting official yet."

"Dad, I didn't quit," she said softly. "Lori fired me. And you let her."

Her father showed a hint of a smile for the first time all evening. "That's because you had it coming! Making calls about *quince* shoes in my office! Dance lessons in City Hall!"

Alicia could feel her heart beating faster. Maybe Maribelle was right—maybe she could fix the situation.

"Actually, I was—" Alicia started to explain, but Maribelle was standing behind her parents, motioning for her to zip it.

"So, Dad, will you rehire me?"

"Well . . . okay. One more chance," he said. "We'll consider it a trial period."

"That's all I need," Alicia said.

• • •

The next morning, Alicia set her alarm clock for five a.m. She'd laid out her clothes the night before—a crisp white button-down shirt with three-quarter-inch sleeves and a red and white toile skirt that Jamie had scored for her on eBay. She didn't know how Jamie had found the vintage items, but it had been a gift. Anytime Alicia went to the Salvation Army or on eBay, all she ever found was junk. She got dressed quickly and didn't bother to blow-dry her hair. She couldn't risk waking her parents up with the noise. Then she grabbed a can of mango juice and a banana and dashed off to make the bus.

By the time her father arrived at the office, she'd done a week's worth of filing, restocked all of his dwindling office supplies, read through ten proposals for video shoots, and signed his name on 150 form letters to constituents. She'd even had time to pick him up a doppio espresso at Starbucks.

"How long have you been here?" he asked.

"I got in early," she said proudly.

"Well, you've certainly gotten a lot done," he said. "But Lici, let me tell you right now. If tomorrow you're back to your same old ways, I'm going to be very disappointed."

Alicia took a deep breath. "The last thing in the world I want to do is disappoint you, Dad." And although she knew it wasn't standard internship behavior, she gave her father a hug.

• • •

Later that afternoon, her internship duties completed, Alicia made her way to the bus stop. She had her phone in her hand and was about to call Carmen to begin her apologies. Suddenly it rang. Looking down at the screen, she smiled. It was Carmen.

"C., I'm so sorry I went all *quince*-crazy," Alicia said before her friend could even say hello.

"No worries," Carmen said. "I've already forgiven you. I figured it was just temporary insanity."

"Something like that," Alicia said, smiling.

"Guess where I am?" Carmen asked.

"No idea," Alicia said.

"Outside the DiaNoches boutique," Carmen said. At least once a month, Carmen visited all the high-end boutiques in town and took notes about the latest trends in designer clothing. "And Sarita's inside. It looks like she's being brainwashed by some fembot salesgirl."

"Don't move," Alicia said. "I'm on my way."

Half an hour later, Alicia and Carmen walked into DiaNoches. Alicia was glad that she had on her internship clothes; they made her feel—and, she hoped, look—more businesslike.

Sarita was standing on the runway, where the owners sometimes staged fashion shows. She was wearing a truly hideous poufy teal green dress that made her look like a mermaid. She was also wearing a blond wig. The end result? She looked *busted*.

"Why is Sarita wearing a wig?" Carmen whispered.

"Long story," Alicia whispered back.

Just then, Sarita turned. Seeing Alicia, her face filled with fury. "What are you doing here?" she screamed. "Did you come to cut off the rest of my hair?"

"You cut her hair?" Carmen asked. She wasn't whispering this time.

"Yes, she scalped me!" Sarita said, ripping off the wig. "She made me bald for my *quinceañera. Esta tipa está loca. ¡Nunca en mi vida he encontrado una chica tan exigente y mandona!*"

Carmen was still dumbfounded. "You *cut* her hair?" she repeated.

"I can explain that," Alicia muttered, mortified anew by her own *quince*-zilla behavior.

"What were you thinking?" Carmen gasped.

Of all the things that had gone wrong in the past forty-eight hours, more than anything, Alicia wished she could have made that particular incident go away.

"I was going for Natalie Portman in *V for Vendetta*," she whispered to Carmen.

The salesgirls were all cracking up. "You cut this poor *chica*'s hair," one of them, named Karina, cackled.

Alicia thought she was going to cry. Nobody seemed

to understand—she had just been trying to help Sarita! "I didn't shave her head," she mumbled. "I just snipped it with the scissors."

"'Snipped it'!" Sarita said, pointing to the bald spot. "*Fíjate. Mira lo que tú has hecho. ¡Esperé este día toda mi vida, mis quince, y tú me cortas el pelo!*"

Suddenly something inside Alicia clicked, and she found her *confianza*. She needed to stand up for what she knew was right.

"Sarita, look in the mirror," Alicia said. "Is that the super-smart, supercute chicana who wants to pilot spaceships one day? This mermaid thing isn't you. I know I went off the deep end for a minute. But I promise you that if you give Amigas Inc. another chance, if you give *me* another chance, I will listen more than I talk. And we—me, Jamie, Carmen, and Gaz—will work night and day to give you the *quince* of your dreams."

Sarita turned to look at herself in the mirror.

Alicia walked up to the runway. "The *quince* of *your* dreams," she repeated. "Not *my* dreams."

Sarita did not look at Alicia. Instead, she stepped down from the raised stage and walked up to Karina.

"Thanks for everything," she said. "But she's right, this isn't me."

"Let's try another dress." Karina suggested.

"It's not the dress."

"You don't like the Little Mermaid theme," Karina said. "I'm cool with that. We can do something different. 'Pirates of the Caribbean' or 'Aladdin.'"

Ignoring Karina, Sarita finally turned to Alicia. "Can we talk for a minute, alone?" she asked.

Alicia nodded, and they walked to the side of the store.

"I'm only going to have one *quince*, and you nearly ruined it," Sarita said. "How can I trust you again?"

A pained expression came over Alicia's face. "I know, I know, it was bad. I'm sorry."

Sarita's eyes flashed. "*Sorry* didn't do it, *you* did."

Alicia grimaced. The past few days had taught her at least one thing—making amends was hard. She took a deep breath and said, "It's because I want you to have the best *quince* ever that I went so crazy," she began. "Honestly, I never knew how many decisions went into every single little bit of it, from the dress to the food to the choreography to the location. Somehow, in trying to keep all the details straight, I lost sight of the most important thing. It's *your* decision. It's *your quince*. At the end of the day, I work for *you*. And I really, really would love to work for you."

Sarita didn't say anything for what felt like forever. Then she extended her hand for Alicia to shake.

"One more chance," Sarita said.

Alicia thought she might cry. "Thank you, thank you, thank you." She reached out to give Sarita a hug, but the girl pulled back.

"No hugging until you figure out what to do about my hair."

"We'll call Jamie," Alicia said. "Jamie will know exactly what to do."

CHAPTER 14

THE GIRLS—Alicia, Sarita, Jamie, and Carmen—were walking down Collins Avenue to a salon so exclusive that it didn't even have a sign, just a jet black door with a shiny silver handle in the center of it. Gaz had bowed out of the mission, once again reminding them, "I'm a guy." It didn't matter. For this, they didn't need him.

Reaching to open the door, Jamie paused and turned to Alicia. "You are so lucky I accepted your apology," she said. "This is going to blow your mind."

The new, humble Alicia took this in stride. "I can't really defend myself, but before you say anything else, just think of all the junk I've taken from you and how I've gotten past it!" Smiling, she pushed past Jamie, and they entered the salon.

The reception area was covered with silver wallpaper, and the chairs were silver, too, with purple velvet cushions. Behind a high desk, a tall, skinny girl with Tyra bangs and bottle green eyes looked them up and down.

"And you are here to see . . . ?" she asked. Alicia couldn't help noticing how a British accent could make you seem snotty, even if you weren't.

"El Vez," Jamie replied.

"Third floor," the girl said, looking impressed in spite of herself.

They piled into the elevator, trying to play it cool. But the minute the elevator doors closed, they all burst out giggling.

"Does he really do Christina Aguilera's hair?" Sarita asked when they'd stopped laughing.

"Yes, he does," Jamie said.

"And he's going to do my hair for free?"

"Yep," Jamie said. "El Vez and my cousin Anton used to be roommates on the Lower East Side. Back when he was just starting out, my cousin—he's a manager at this store called Jeffrey now—got El Vez his first gig doing Chloë Sevigny's hair for a movie premiere. He comes to South Beach for one week every month. He's always offering to hook me up, as a favor to my cousin. But as you can see, there's nothing a professional can do for me that I can't do for myself."

Jamie was completely right—if not modest.

"I'm a little nervous," Sarita said, as the elevator doors opened and they walked into the sunny loft space.

"Don't be," Alicia said. "We've got our inspiration photo, and this time we're all on the same page."

"What's that actress's name again?" Carmen asked, looking at the picture.

"Catherine Deneuve," said Sarita. "From *Umbrellas of Cherbourg*. It's one of my mom's and my favorite movies."

"But it's not going to be blond, right?" Alicia said.

Just then, El Vez walked up to them. "Blond, no. Not on a beautiful *morena* like you," he said, kissing Sarita's hand. "You must be Sarita. Jamie e-mailed me a picture of you. But it doesn't do you justice. Has anyone ever told you that you look like a young Salma Hayek?"

Sarita turned bright red. "Get out!" she squealed.

El Vez just laughed. He was tall and thin with a mop of hair that looked like Shaggy's from *Scooby-Doo*, if Shaggy had had his hair precision-cut and rocked a very neat goatee, that is.

"Jamie, my love," he said, giving his old friend a kiss on both cheeks.

"Be careful with him," Jamie warned the group. "He's a massive flirt."

"I don't mind!" Sarita said.

"But I bet Diego, your *chambelán*, would," Alicia said. "Does he still hate me? Have I traumatized him for life about your dance number?"

"Nah," Sarita said. "He doesn't scare that easy."

Alicia smiled and introduced herself and Carmen to El Vez.

"*Mucho gusto*," El Vez said. "Okay, let's get down to business, because extensions take time. I understand you have an inspiration photo."

"I do," Sarita said. "The French actress Catherine Deneuve—"

"From *The Umbrellas of Cherbourg*." El Vez and Sarita said the movie title at the same time, gazing at the photo with the same adoration.

"A girl who loves old movies! We're going to get along just fine," El Vez said, taking Sarita's hand. He then turned to assess the group. "There are too many cooks in this kitchen. Who's staying, and who's *going*?"

"*I'm* going," Jamie said. "There's a consignment shop in Hallandale where they are holding a pair of high-heeled Timberlands for me. I think they might be perfect for Sarita's opening dance. You're a size six, right?"

"Right," said Sarita.

"And I've got to go to a costume shop in the Gables to see if I can find some mariachi outfits for Gaz's band," said Carmen.

"I'll hang out a little bit," Alicia said. "How about we all meet back at my place around five?"

"Sounds good," Carmen said.

"It's a plan," Jamie agreed.

As she watched her friends leave, Alicia couldn't help feeling lucky that she and her girls were back on speaking terms again. Things were moving much more smoothly now.

As Sarita and Alicia peppered El Vez with questions about being on tour with Christina Aguilera, he got to work on Sarita's hair.

"Is she nice?" Sarita wanted to know.

"Does she really have such beautiful skin?" asked Alicia. She'd had a really bad case of eczema in the fifth grade and had been obsessed with skin care ever since.

"Is she really blond?" asked Sarita.

"Does she sing while you do her hair?" Alicia wondered.

El Vez smiled slyly. "You know what they say. A gentleman never tells."

He went on to explain that the extensions he was using were of the best quality and should last six to eight weeks.

Sarita did a little jump for joy. "That means I'll still be rocking them when school starts. Talk about more bounce to the diva ounce."

As Sarita and El Vez continued to chat, Alicia carefully studied the checklist in her folder. It never hurt to be prepared.

> Beach permit – ✓
> Band – ✓
> Mariachi music and costumes for Jaz – ✓

Sarita's dress – ✓
Sarita's heels – *coming*
Damas' dresses – ✓
Chambelanes' suits – ✓
Sets – ✓
Church ceremony – ✓

She paused and remembered how Maribelle had told her that a *quince* should be much more than a party. Sarita's mom had volunteered to make the church arrangements, so Alicia hadn't given it a second thought. But now that she'd gotten to know Sarita, she was curious about how the religious ceremony would tie together all that followed.

"Do you and your mom go to church every Sunday?" Alicia asked as El Vez sewed in a row of long, silky extensions.

"Not really," Sarita said. "My mom has her museum events on the weekends. But we do go to Saturday evening mass sometimes, and we both love it. My mom says no matter what you believe, it's a beautiful ritual—the singing, the candles, the communion. And rituals are what give our life meaning."

Alicia thought about the rituals in her life: her parents' annual Winter Wonderland party; the Saturday movie nights they'd been having since she was a kid; and Christmas, when no one opened a single present until Maribelle made hot cross buns, which she called Jesus's birthday cake, and someone blew out the candle and made a wish on Jesus's behalf.

Rituals *did* add meaning to life, and it was her job to make sure that Sarita's *quinceañera* was the most important ritual the girl had ever had.

"Have you written your vows?" Alicia asked.

In the old days, girls had merely repeated the church's vows. Maribelle said that when she was a *quince*, she had had to say hers in Latin. But these days, girls wrote their own, reflecting the people and the things that were most important to them. Of course, this whole write-your-own-vows thing did not always work out.

At one church ceremony Alicia had attended, the girl had used her vows to discuss the role of fashion in her life. It had been an absolutely idiotic speech about how when she was in middle school, she had worn a lot of Baby Phat and Harajuku Lovers, but now that she was a *quince*, and coming into her own, she was proudly wearing labels like Shoshanna, Tracy Reese, and Kors by Michael Kors. She then went on to say that she looked forward to embracing more fashion-forward designers like Narciso Rodriguez and Zac Posen. It had been the most superficial, name-droppy church ceremony Alicia had ever seen. She'd even overhead her dad talking about how the priest had taken the girl's parents aside and criticized them for not vetting her speech and making sure she understood the meaning of the vows. Alicia happily retold that story now, and Sarita laughed at the girl's fashion litany.

"Well, I won't be going that route," Sarita said. "Mostly because my mom would tar and feather me, stake me to a canvas, and call it art. I'm just going to thank my mom for always sacrificing so I could have everything, even when that means she doesn't have as much. I'm going to thank my dad for teaching me that family is still family, even after a divorce. And I'll throw in some kiss-up remarks to my *tías*, because they're bitter and vindictive, and they'll do nothing but *chismear* about me if I don't."

"That sounds great, *chica*," Alicia said, standing up and giving Sarita a hug. "It looks like you are in great hands, and there is still lots to do. I'm going to jet, but I'll see you and your guy at dance rehearsal tomorrow night."

"We'll be there," Sarita said. "What about the cake-tasting? My mom's been asking about it."

Alicia felt all the color drain out of her face. The cake! *She'd totally forgotten about the cake!* But no big deal, she thought. It was only a cake. Maribelle could make one in her sleep.

"I'm all over it," Alicia said with confidence. "Today's Tuesday. The *quinceañera* is Saturday. How about we do the cake-tasting at your mom's job on Thursday?"

"Sounds good," Sarita said. "And thank you for this." She fingered her new raven locks.

"You're welcome," Alicia said. "You deserve it."

• • •

Alicia's confidence was quickly shattered.

"I don't do cakes," Maribelle said when Alicia brought it up.

"Of course you do," Alicia said. "You're an amazing cook."

"Thank you very much. I know that I am," Maribelle said. "Which is why I know that cooking and baking are not the same thing. Think about it. When have you ever seen me bake a cake?"

"You make flan!"

"Not baking," Maribelle said.

"And crème brûlée!"

"I love the little blowtorch," Maribelle said. "But that is not baking."

"What about your famous chocolate-chip cookies?" Alicia asked. "That *is* baking."

Maribelle looked guilty. "I follow the recipe on the Toll House chips bag, and I add shaved coconut to give it the Maribelle touch."

"You don't!"

"I do!" Maribelle said. "Don't tell your brother."

Alicia sighed. "So we just follow a cake recipe. We'll do it together. I can help. How hard could it be?"

Maribelle huffed. "Hard! I'm already making dinner on the beach for two hundred people. I will not be making the cake. I do not have the time, the energy, or the desire."

"But our budget is stretched to the max," Alicia said imploringly.

"Then you are going to have to crack open your piggy bank, because a professionally made cake is very expensive."

Alicia sat down at the kitchen counter. "I know," she said with a sigh. "I priced them. We're talking eight hundred, nine hundred bucks for a *quince* cake, and that's if we do a cake that feeds a hundred and supplement it with a sheet cake for the other hundred people." Alicia looked up at Maribelle. "You know what? I'll just have to make it myself."

Maribelle laughed. "Ha! I'm going to watch my *novela*, where the deluded women are played by real actresses, not ambitious teenagers."

As Alicia went through Maribelle's cookbooks, looking for a cake recipe, she thought: It's my job to make sure that Sarita has the best *quince* Miami has ever seen. And that means the best cake—like a giant one in the shape of a rocket ship.

Unfortunately, Maribelle's cookbooks were a little short on rocket-ship-shaped cake recipes, so she flipped open her laptop and searched for a recipe online.

Hmm, she thought. Google has ninety-four thousand eight hundred results for rocket-ship cake. Sarita will be done with college and working at NASA before I get through all of these.

She went to her father's office and printed out a picture

of the most realistic-looking one. Then she called Carmen, Gaz, and Alicia to ask them to scratch coming over that night. She needed them to come over in the morning instead and help. She found a recipe for an ambrosia cake that sounded delicious (coconut flakes, banana and orange filling, *yum*). Then she divided the grocery list among the crew, so that everyone could play a part, and sent them an e-mail. Gaz would go to the cake-decorating shop for sparklers, silver balls, and all the decorations they would need to make the cake's base. Carmen would head to the Coconut Grove farmers' market for butter, eggs, oranges, and milk. And Jamie would hit up Half Moon Empanadas for their bacon, egg, and cheese breakfast empanadas, so they wouldn't be eating batter all morning long.

The next morning, promptly at ten, everyone arrived. Maribelle sat at the kitchen counter with her cup of coffee.

"This is something I've got to see," she said with a chuckle.

All of the *amigas*—and Gaz—moved around the Cruzes' kitchen as if it were their own. Over the years, they'd spent so much time there it felt like an extension of home. It wasn't just where they chowed down on Maribelle's greatest culinary hits; the Cruz kitchen was where they baked cookies after school in junior high, where they made popcorn on movie nights, and made Cuban pressed sandwiches with the family's thousand-dollar, restaurant-quality panini grill.

A sleepy Jamie reached for a square ceramic platter, her eyes still half closed, and put the breakfast empanadas on them.

"You're not going to warm them?" Maribelle looked genuinely horrified. "Who eats cold empanadas?"

"No te preocupes," Gaz told her, taking the empanadas and sliding them off the platter into a pan and then popping them into the oven, which he set for 350 degrees. "I'll warm 'em up."

Jamie poured herself a cup of coffee from the old-fashioned silver pot that sat on the stove. "How many *amigas* does it take to bake a cake, anyway? Can't I go back to bed?"

Alicia, who was dressed in a turquoise one-shoulder T-shirt and orange cutoffs, shook her head. "All four of us," she said. "This is more than a cake; it's a team-building exercise, a *symbol* of what Amigas really is, a *monument* to our swagger, made of sugar and flour. "

Jamie sat down next to Maribelle at the kitchen counter and rolled her eyes. "Whatever. I'll take my slice of symbol or monument or whatever to go."

"Escucha esta tontería!" Maribelle giggled. "I love it."

Carmen was studying the color printout of the rocket-ship cake. "This looks complicated, Lici," she said. "Where'd you get this picture?"

"From the Web site of a bakery in New York," Alicia explained. "Sylvia Weinstock."

"She's a *very* famous pastry chef," Jamie added. "I read about her in *New York* magazine."

"So? What's the big deal, Miss New York?" Alicia said. "You're on butter-and-sugar duty. You should like that, because you can do it sitting down."

Alicia plopped the family's cherry red mixer down in front of Jamie.

"I do like it," Jamie said, perking up. "It even matches." As Jamie was wearing a lipstick red Japanese-style obi belt over a ribbed white boyfriend T, this was absolutely and categorically true.

Carmen, who thought of cooking as analogous to sewing, was doing what she always did when she began a big project—arranging all her material. She was the only one of the *amigas* to be wearing a proper apron, which she'd made herself out of vintage fabric she'd found online. Alicia was pretty sure that her grandmother had wallpaper in the same exact blue and orange pattern. But on Carmen, it looked more than acceptable, it looked cool.

First, Carmen lined up all the ingredients for the cake: baking powder, salt, butter, sugar, eggs, vanilla, and whole milk. She raised an eyebrow. There were a couple of things missing. "We don't have self-rising flour," Carmen told Alicia.

"No problem," Alicia said, as she whisked together eggs for the filling. "We'll just add more baking powder."

"Ha!" Maribelle said.

"And we don't have orange zest," Carmen said.

"I don't even know what orange zest is," Gaz said. He was engaged in the very manly task of buttering the pans.

"No problem," Alicia said. "We'll use a little bit of orange juice."

"Ha!" Maribelle said again.

"Are you going to be doing that all day?" Alicia asked, trying to keep the irritation out of her voice.

Maribelle nodded yes.

"Gre-e-e-eat," Alicia said.

Then it all started to go horribly, terribly, regrettably wrong. In an effort to soften the butter, which someone had accidentally put in the freezer, Alicia microwaved it. For three minutes.

"Oh, my God, it stinks!" Carmen said, opening up the microwave and fanning the burning butter wildly.

"Open a door!" Gaz said.

Alicia ran over to the door between the kitchen and the pool. "Who knew that a little bit of butter could smell so bad?"

"I knew," Maribelle said.

Alicia glared at her.

Jamie began beating the butter and sugar, but it quickly became apparent that the mixer was broken, because it made a huge clanking noise like the noise of a muffler dragging off the tail end of a very old car.

"The bowl's too big," Gaz surmised after giving it the guy once-over.

"You think?" Maribelle said.

"But that's the bowl that comes with it," Alicia said.

"Nah," Gaz said, kneeling down to check the cabinets in the center of the kitchen island. "You need a wooden bowl, Jamie. My Mom always mixes butter and sugar in a wooden bowl."

Jamie scraped the contents of the metal bowl into the wooden bowl and turned the mixer on, and it splattered everywhere. The butter-and-sugar concoction covered every wall of the kitchen and landed in significant globs in Alicia's hair.

"Nice work, Jamie," Alicia grumbled. She was getting crankier by the second.

They scraped what was left from the wooden bowl and added the other ingredients.

"How much do you think we lost on the walls?" Carmen asked.

"Not much," Alicia said, mixing it all together. "It looks good. Who wants to lick the spoon?"

Gaz did. But the moment he tasted it, he made a sour face. "Needs more sugar. And it's kinda dry."

"It probably needs more butter," Carmen advised.

"Okay, fine," Alicia said. "Jamie, can you microwave this stick of butter for thirty seconds?"

"Okay," Jamie said. "But maybe I should do it on the stove top. The microwave still smells like burned popcorn."

"Microwave is faster," Alicia said. "Time is money."

She added a cup of honey to the batter.

Maribelle, who had been very quiet for a while, said, "May I ask about the honey?"

"Well, Gaz said it was dry. So instead of adding more sugar, I'm adding honey."

Jamie added the melted butter to the batter and mixed it all in.

"Okay, Gaz," she said, handing him a fresh spoon. "Taste test."

"Tastes good," he said, nodding slowly. He had been expecting something inedible.

"Excellent," Alicia said proudly.

They put the cake in the oven for twenty-five minutes, and then Jamie took it out.

"It looks kind of pathetic," she said, staring at the shrunken yellow cake.

"It just needs more time," Carmen said enthusiastically as she set the oven timer for an additional fifteen minutes.

Fifteen minutes later, it had fallen in on itself. Carmen took it out.

"It doesn't look like a cake. It looks like a soufflé," she said.

"A soufflé that is having a really, really rough day," Alicia added.

Finally, Maribelle stood up. "May I speak?" she asked.

"Sure," Alicia said, leaning her head on Maribelle's shoulder. "Tell us what we did wrong."

"There's no use in rehashing the past," Maribelle said. "But I will tell you that the time has come to do the right thing."

"And what is that?" Alicia asked.

"Put this disaster out of its misery, and buy that poor *quince* girl a proper cake."

It took them more than an hour to clean up. In the meantime, Maribelle took the ambrosia filling and made a topping for ice-cream sundaes, which they scarfed down with abandon. It was nearly two o'clock when Gaz, Carmen, and Jamie walked out the door.

"At least we tried," Carmen said. "I may not know how to make a cake, but I can promise you that Sarita's dresses will be bangin'."

Jamie did a little dance move. "And I, for one, can't wait to get my groove on."

Gaz said, "You and me both." Then he turned to Alicia. "On my way in to work this afternoon, I'll stop back by the cake-supply shop."

"Do you think they'll take back the eight hundred silver beads we bought to make rivets on the rocket ship?" Alicia asked hopefully.

"No," Gaz said. "Especially since we used about fifty of them on our sundaes. But I'll tell them we need a fast and affordable cake baker and see what they say."

"Thanks," Alicia said and reached up to give him the half hug, half peck on the cheek that had become their regular hello and good-bye. She felt a familiar pang and wondered why he didn't just kiss her. On TV and in the movies, teen-age boys couldn't wait to plant one on you. It was as if they didn't know what else to do with their lips. In real life, at least in her experience, even when a boy liked you and he knew you liked him back, he still took his sweet time.

Just as Gaz and the girls drove away, Alex pulled up.

"Just the party-planner I wanted to see," her brother said. "We have a problem with the set."

"Problem? Please don't say the word *problem* to me," Alicia said, following him back into the house.

"I've got a problem, but I've also got a solution," Alex retorted, as he poured himself a tall glass of milk.

"Excellent," Alicia said. "I *love* solutions."

"You know how after Sarita's big dance number she's supposed to crawl into the spaceship and the stage fills with smoke?"

"Yep."

"Well, there's no smoke. City ordinance. Smoke machines aren't allowed in high-density public places. People think there's a fire, they stampede, and folks get hurt."

Alicia could not believe her ears. "No one's going to stampede because they see smoke at a beach," she said. "We're right next to the ocean! Even if there was a fire, we'd be perfectly safe."

"You'd think," Alex said. "But the guy at the city council was pretty adamant. No smoke machines on the beach."

Alicia groaned. "You said you had a solution?"

Alex smiled. "Bubbles," he said mysteriously.

"Bubbles? They're so-o-o infantile."

Now it was Alex's turn to roll his eyes. "And having a girl pretend to be an astronaut and climbing into a spaceship is really serious and mature."

"Point taken," Alicia said. "Let me think about it, okay?"

"Don't think too hard," Alex said, as he headed back to his room. "If I want it for Saturday, I've got to reserve the bubble machine in the morning."

CHAPTER 15

ALICIA NEEDED TIME to recharge. Heading upstairs, she walked into her room and promptly lay down—on the floor. "Fudge, fudge, fudge," she whispered into the ground.

She had problems. She had huge, insurmountable problems. She had no cake. She had no smoke machine. And she only had a few days left. How was she going to tell Sarita?

At that moment, her dad walked into the room. "Lici, I see you got my message," he said, taking in her prone figure. "Don't worry, we'll figure something out."

Alicia sat up. "What message?"

"I left you three messages on your cell phone."

"I didn't get them."

Her dad looked concerned. "Well, I got a call from my buddy in the city-planning department. He saw there was a problem with your beach permit for the *quince* on Saturday."

Alicia felt as though she'd just been slapped. "No way," she said. "I filed that permit weeks ago."

Her father reached into his shirt pocket. He looked sad. While he could be tough when he needed to be, he hated to be the bearer of bad news. "I know, Lici, but you filed the wrong form. This is for a public event."

"Right."

"But a *quinceañera* is not a public event, it's a private one."

Alicia was pretty sure that if her life had been a movie, this would have been the part where the judge asked her if she had any last requests before she made the long walk to the electric chair.

She let herself fall into her father's arms and buried her face in his chest as the tears started to flow uncontrollably. It was all falling apart.

"Dad," she asked through her tears, "how is a party not a public event?"

"I'm sorry, *hija*. I wish you had asked for my help when you were filling out the forms. A public event is open to people on the street, like a Cinco de Mayo festival or the Art Fair. A party with a select guest list is a private event."

Alicia tried to compose herself. "So all I have to do is fill out the right form and . . ."

Her father got that Bad News Bears look on his face again. "Unfortunately, the area where you wanted to have the *quince* has been reserved by a group that filled out the right form."

Alicia groaned. "Who? Maybe if I talk to them?"

"The group is called VOCUFANA."

"Voca-who?"

Her father shook his head. "It's the Veterans of Color United in Faith for a New Administration summer social. They're a bunch of tough old military guys who don't take no for an answer. Besides, they served our country honorably. You should let them have their picnic."

"Dad, what am I going to do?"

Her father smiled. "Well, when I couldn't reach you on the phone I took the liberty of filing a permit for you at another location."

"Great. Where?"

"Pier Seventeen," he said.

"In front of the Coronado hotel?" Alicia asked.

He nodded. "It seemed like a good choice," he said. "It's near a lot of public transportation, and there's a taxi stand at the hotel, in case some of the older relatives want to go home early."

"Oh, Dad," Alicia sighed.

"Did I not do good?" her father asked.

"No, you did great. It's a perfect choice," Alicia said, kissing him on the forehead.

• • •

After her dad left, Alicia called Sarita.

"Hey, Sarita," Alicia said. "Everything's good, but there have been some developments. Would it be okay if I came over to talk to you and your mom?"

"Sure," Sarita said.

Alicia told her she'd be right over. Then she went to find her mom. She needed a ride.

It felt like ages since Alicia and her mother had had any time alone. Before Gaz and Alex had their licenses, it had always been her mom who shuttled her to dance classes and play rehearsals, and to the mall, last summer, when she, Jamie, and Carmen had worked at Cinnabon.

"Lici," her mom said once they'd gotten in the car, "I want you to know how proud I am that you turned things around with your internship."

"Thanks, Mom," Alicia said, smiling happily. At least that was going well. She *had* been trying. Even though she could have ridden in to work with her dad, Alicia still got up early every morning and took the bus. By the time her father arrived at the office, Alicia would have been there for over an hour, and she always had a doppio espresso waiting for him. And to Alicia's surprise, she discovered that when she actually paid attention, there was a lot of cool stuff about the way her city was run. She was working hard, but it was worth it. It seemed her *quince* year was really turning into the grown-up transition that Maribelle had hinted it could be.

Sarita and her mom lived in a beautiful old art deco apartment building in the historic part of the Gables. Alicia had assumed that her own mom would wait in the car and go over court documents, which is what she always did when she drove Alicia to dance class. But this time it was different. "Actually, I'd like to come in and meet the lucky lady whom my daughter is working so hard for," she said when they arrived.

Standing in Sarita's living room, Alicia couldn't help noticing how different the two moms were. Alicia's mom was short and reed thin, and, despite her height, she cut an imposing figure in her four-inch Manolo heels and razor-cut bob. Sarita's mom was taller, with waist-length hair that reminded Alicia of Rapunzel's. She had almond-shaped eyes that were rimmed with black eyeliner, and big gold hoops hung from her ears. She was wearing an embroidered green Chinese jacket, a white T-shirt, and jeans. Even barefoot, she loomed a good six inches above both Alicia and her mom.

After everyone was introduced, Alicia took out her Amigas binder, which not only had her checklist, but all of the contact info for the vendors, as well as the receipts and delivery schedules.

"I feel like I haven't been looping you in on all the major decisions the way I should have," Alicia said. "I've made some choices in an effort to save money. . . ."

Sarita looked embarrassed. "I know, our budget isn't very big."

"No, Sarita. Your budget is just fine. I've just been acting like it's my *quince*, and it's not, it's your *quince*. And while I thought I knew how to make it perfect, the truth is that it doesn't have to be perfect for me, it's got to be perfect for *you*." Alicia was slightly flustered. It was tougher than she thought being in charge of something as important as somebody's *quince*. She took a deep breath and started again. "I thought I could make your *quince* cake, and it was kind of a disaster, so we're going to have to buy you one instead."

Sarita didn't look upset. "That's fine."

"There's more," Alicia went on. "I messed up your beach permit, so we lost our location."

Sarita *did* look slightly upset at this.

"But, my dad filled out another one, and we'll have it on the beach, in front of the Coronado hotel. It's an even better spot, because it's really central, lots of taxicabs for your guests."

"Okay," Sarita said warily.

"And Gaz's band has offered to play, as you know," Alicia

continued. She turned to Sarita's mother. "I've brought along a CD for you to check out. This is his original music. But they've also offered to do covers, too—classic salsa, reggaeton. And, as Sarita and I have discussed, they'll be doing a merengue number for the father-daughter dance."

She handed the CD to Sarita's mom.

"Why don't you pop the CD in, Sari?" Ms. Lopez said.

Gaz's sweet alto filled the Lopezes' living room. Alicia loved his music, but she wasn't sure if part of that was because she was also in love with him. "What do you think?" she asked nervously.

"I've always said it's the hotness," Sarita said. "Mom?"

Her mother laughed. "The *quince* has spoken."

Alicia's mother smiled. "I had no idea how talented Gaz was. If only I'd known that the boy who has been eating me out of house and home was the next Enrique Iglesias, I would've fed him even more!"

Alicia smiled. "He *is* really good."

"And really cute," Sarita chimed in.

"Was Gaz the lead *chambelán* for your *quince*?" Ms. Lopez asked.

Gaz her *chambelán*? That would have been dreamy. Maybe if she'd had a *quince*, she and Gaz would have been dating by now. Your *chambelán* was supposed to be somebody platonic, a second cousin or a family friend, someone

172

you could count on to learn the dances and behave in front of your family, without any drama. But Alicia had been to enough *quinces* to know that a *chambelán* could start as a friend and end up as much more.

Alicia stole a quick glance at her mom. "Um, I didn't have a *quince*. My mom and dad took me and my best friend to Spain instead."

"Wow, Spain," Sarita's mom said. "I can't wait to take Sarita to Bilbao. That's what next year's savings account will be targeted for."

"Ms. Lopez, I know how hard you've worked to make Sarita's *quince* possible," Alicia said. "Amigas is working hard to make sure that this is a day Sarita will never ever forget."

"I appreciate that," Ms. Lopez said.

"Me, too," Sarita said. She tossed her long hair. "It's not even my *quince* yet, and I already feel like a movie star."

Driving home, Alicia felt better than she had in a long time. Despite the ups—and lots of downs—things were looking better. Her mom turned to look at her. "Okay," Mrs. Cruz said. "What did you do with my little Lici? You've taken her away and replaced her with this formidable business-woman."

Alicia smiled. "I'm still your Lici. And Alex's Squeak. And dad's intern. Just to prove how down to earth I am, I'll let you buy me a scoop of rum raisin in a chocolate-covered cone on our way home."

Her mom turned right, guiding the car on the route that led past the Coral Gables soda shop and ice-cream parlor. "It would be an honor, Alicia."

CHAPTER 16

THE MORNING of Sarita's *quinceañera*, Alicia woke early, a big smile on her face and her heart beating wildly, as if it were Christmas instead of an ordinary Saturday morning in the summer. The church ceremony would not start until three in the afternoon, but it seemed to Alicia that even with nine hours at her disposal, there was no way she could get it all done. She got out of bed and threw on an old sundress that had been her mom's. It was made of silk scarves, each printed with a part of the map of the Florida. Her mother called the dress *basura*, but Alicia knew that it wasn't trash; it was her lucky charm.

She was not surprised to find Maribelle cooking in the kitchen, even though the sun was barely up. Maribelle was wearing a yellow housedress and a bright orange apron that read: *Dale besitos al cocinera.*

She smiled at Alicia. "How are you doing, sleepyhead?"

Alicia feigned being offended. "You're killing me. It's not even six yet."

"And I have been up since four thirty," Maribelle pointed out.

"That's why I got up early," Alicia said. "So I could help you."

Maribelle raised an eyebrow. "I like the new and improved Lici. Here's a knife. You start peeling plaintains, and I will make you a smoothie."

While Maribelle and Alicia cooked, Jamie was also up bright and early. She had two hundred party favors to finish before noon, when she was due at Sarita's to style her hair and makeup. She was hooking up not only Sarita, but also her mom and all seven of her *damas*.

As her family slept, Jamie made herself a toasted English muffin and spread it with rose jelly that her grandmother had sent from the Bronx.

Looking at all the party-favor elements laid out in the living room, she had to admit that it was pretty genius. She'd had the science museum order two hundred envelopes of astronaut ice cream. Then she'd taken several photos of Sarita, post–Christina Aguilera extensions, and placed them over pics of Lily Allen dressed like an astronaut in an old Common video. It had come out even more amazing than she'd hoped. The supersaturated colors of the video really popped with Sarita's rich black hair and the huge false eyelashes that Jamie had put on her. In the photos, she looked like Penélope Cruz or Eva Mendes.

As a final touch, Jamie had the Sarita astronaut pics made into five-by-seven stickers at Kinko's. All she had to do now was to cover the label of the astronaut ice cream with Sarita's astronaut stickers. She'd saved it for Saturday morning, because she hadn't thought it would take so long, but as she carefully peeled off each sticker and affixed it to the ice cream, she worried that this might have been a bad idea. "I hope someone wakes up soon," she mumbled, "because this *chica* could really use a hand."

Over by the canals, Carmen's house was already buzzing. The twins rarely slept past seven, and they made such a racket racing up and down the stairs that nobody else did, either. Carmen's stepfather was in the kitchen making pan after pan of blueberry muffins. Carmen had thought she was in the clear with Sarita's party dress, but at the last fitting, it had been a little tight in the hips. She wanted Sarita to feel ultraconfident on the dance floor, so she'd let out the dress and started again. The machine sewing had gone quickly, but the sequins had had to be sewn by hand, and the silver-netting flounces were slippery to work with. Carmen wolfed down a muffin and a strong cup of *café con leche* and made her way to her favorite window seat. One sequin, two sequins, only two hundred and ninety-seven sequins to go . . .

• • •

While the girls were all up early, the morning of Sarita's *quince* didn't have quite the same effect on the lone guy in the group. Gaz was sleeping soundly. He and his brothers had been up until three in the morning, rehearsing the songs they'd planned to play. While they had had a blast rocking out to songs by Shakira, Alejandro Sanz, Marc Anthony, and Daddy Yankee, the truth was, they were all a little nervous. It was one thing to play your own music, but it was quite another to do an acceptable job on songs that people knew and loved. Every time Gaz hit the snooze button, he said an impossible prayer for more time to rehearse.

Three p.m. found Amigas Inc. sitting in the last pew of Our Lady of Divine Patience in Coral Gables. Sarita entered in her church dress, a white empire-waist design with cap sleeves that Carmen had modeled after an old Chloé gown she'd seen in a magazine. She'd covered the bottom of the dress with the same silver netting that she'd used on the party dress, and she'd sprinkled a few sequins on the bodice as a hint of what was to come. Watching Sarita walk in, Carmen was proud to see that it hit the right note between modest enough for church and unexpected and cool.

The Amigas were all dressed in black tops and white jeans. It had been Alicia's idea that they should wear some sort of uniform, so that they could be easily identified in a crowd, should anybody need help. They were also all carrying pocketfuls of brand-new Amigas business cards.

They had watched the *quinceañera* church ceremony dozens of times. Had heard the priest bless the girl turning fifteen. Had looked on as the *quince*'s father helped her change from flats to high heels. Had seen the girl read her vows—promising, always, to be a credit to the community and to make her parents proud. In all honesty, they'd been a bit burned out on *quinces*. How many times can you watch the same thing and still find it exciting or even vaguely interesting? But as Sarita's friends and family filled the church, as Sarita walked up to the altar and began the passage into adulthood that was so essential to the Latino *cultura*, each felt as if she were watching the ceremony for the first time. Sarita was not just any *quince*. She was *their quince*.

The feeling was mutual, because at the end of her vows, Sarita looked over to where the group sat and said, "Last but not least, I need to thank Amigas Incorporated, who planned and organized my *quince*. Cinderella had one fairy godmother; I was lucky enough to have four."

Alicia, Jamie, and Carmen broke church protocol and clapped wildly. Only Gaz remained silent.

"This is getting ridiculous," he muttered.

"What?" Alicia said.

"Did you hear her refer to me as a *godmother*?" he fumed.

Alicia couldn't help grinning. He was cute when he was mad.

"It's a metaphor," Alicia whispered.

"It's an insult," Gaz said. He took out the business cards. "And what am I supposed to do with these? I'm not an *amiga*."

"It's a metaphor," Alicia whispered again.

"It's an insult," Gaz repeated.

But Alicia got the sense that he wasn't really mad. She would figure out a way to smooth things out later—after the *quinceañera* was over. They had a *lot* to talk about.

Down at the beach, Maribelle was commanding the troops, made up largely of Alex's friends and Gaz's brothers, with easy confidence. The food had been set up at different stations. Appetizers included empanadas, *croquetas*, plaintain "boats" filled with *ropa vieja*, little *copitas* of ceviche and *tostones con mojo*. There was an entrée table with camarones, pernil, and chicken kebobs. Then there was the dessert table, a tribute to Alicia's utter inability to bake a cake: a wire rocket ship, filled with 200 cupcakes.

Alex and his crew had assembled a platform for the performances, and there was a very realistic-looking spaceship facade made of scrap metal, waiting for Sarita's first dance.

Gaz's brothers set up the favor table with Sarita's party favors and then started work on the sound system.

Shortly after the ceremony ended, guests began to arrive

at the pier, and as the sun set and the waves broke gently in the background, Alicia took to the stage. "Ladies and gentlemen, it's my pleasure to introduce you to our honored *quinceañera*, Sarita Lopez, her *damas* and *chambelanes*."

The step band Alicia had hired began to march down the boardwalk, and everyone looked up at the commotion. Alicia was thrilled. It was just the element of surprise she'd been hoping for. The guys, dressed in their full marching gear, stepped onto the stage and began chanting in their deep voices.

> *Fifteen steps. Fifteen candles. Fifteen souls at bay.*
> *It's a beach party. It's a space party.*
> *'Cause she does it her way.*
> *She's a lady now, can't you see it?*
> *Her beauty will leave you in a haze.*
> *Sarita's working that gown.*
> *Soon she'll be running this town.*
> *They'll be talking 'bout her quince*
> *For days. Days. Days. Days.*

The step band parted, and Sarita stepped forward, dressed in a white lab coat, black-rimmed glasses, and the Timberland boots that Jamie had spray-painted silver. She threw off her coat to reveal the silver minidress that Carmen had designed for her, and the audience went crazy. Lights flashed wildly as everyone snapped the beaming Sarita with whatever they had—video cameras, digital cameras, disposable cameras, and cell phones.

Madonna's "Ray of Light" started to play over the speakers, and the stage filled with bubbles. Alicia chewed her pencil nervously, hoping that none of the *damas* and *chambelanes* forgot the choreography. Someone squeezed her shoulder and she jumped. It was Alex. She smiled up at her big brother.

"You startled me," she said.

"See, told you, the bubbles are wild," he said.

"You were right," Alicia said.

"This really is something," Alex said, looking around. "You did good, Sis. Congrats."

Sarita's guy, Diego, was not the best dancer. Alicia had revised the choreography so he didn't have to do anything but an old hip-hop dance called the Professor. He simply had to wave his hands in the air, then wave them toward the ground. Diego had obviously been practicing, because he moved his hands wildly with something resembling rhythm, a huge smile on his face.

Sarita, it turned out, was quite the dancer despite her fears, torquing her torso with Shakira-like finesse.

Jamie came over and joined Alicia. "She can move."

"I know. Nice job on her hair, her makeup, and especially those shoes. You should have your own TV show, *Pimp My Sneaks.*"

Then Carmen joined them. "No, when I'm a world-famous designer, Jamie should do the exclusive shoes for my show."

"Wait a second," Jamie said. "You're a world-famous designer, I hook up your shoes, and what does that make me?"

Carmen laughed. "That makes you the girl who designs shoes for a world-famous designer."

Jamie shook her head. "Nah, I'll pass," she said, but she was smiling.

After dinner, it was time for the father-daughter *vals*. Alicia had a special surprise for Sarita. Because Alicia had convinced her it was the grown-up thing to do, Sarita thought that she and her dad were going to do a traditional waltz. But ever since her dad, Alfonso, had gotten to town the week before, Alicia had been working with him on a special number.

Jamie introduced Sarita and Alfonso. "Hey, everybody," she bellowed into the mike in her best Bronxese. "Settle down. It's time for the father-daughter *vals.*"

Sarita and her father took to the stage, and Gaz's band moved to the sidelines—except for Gaz, who made an announcement about the song he was about to sing. Alicia started. This wasn't part of the plan. What was Gaz doing?

"This is a new song that I wrote called *'Desde Siempre'*—*Since Forever*," he said, in a soft, deep voice. "I know it probably seems like forever since you've been waiting for your *quince*, Sarita, and it's finally here."

The crowd whooped, hollered, and clapped.

"But *'Desde Siempre'* has another meaning for me," Gaz continued. "This song was inspired by a really good friend of mine, my best friend, in fact."

Alicia looked around to see who Gaz was talking about, even as she hoped it was her. This time, there was no denying it. He was smiling right at her.

Jamie was standing near the catering table, giving her a double thumbs-up, and Carmen, who was helping Alex with the balloons, gave her a big grin.

Gaz's voice cracked just a little, and Alicia could see that the crowd was getting restless. So was she.

"Alicia, this song is called *'Desde Siempre,'* because I've been wanting to tell you, since forever, how much you mean to me and how I really feel about you."

Gaz started to sing, and the rich vibrato of his voice floated down the beach, like waves hitting the shore.

Alicia couldn't move. She couldn't even sway, though the rhythm of the song was sweet and infectious, like Justin

Timberlake meets Alejandro Sanz. Even though she wasn't wearing the dress, and even though all these people hadn't come out to celebrate her, hearing Gaz sing a song that he'd written for her, on the beach, under the moon and the stars, Alicia couldn't help feeling that this was her night, too.

After the father-daughter *vals*, Sarita's father took the microphone to thank her family and friends for joining them all on this special occasion. Gaz made a beeline for Alicia, held her hand, and walked her backstage. Then he kissed her, quickly, softly, gently, *suavemente*. A kiss that left no doubt that it was the first of many more to come.

Then, as though it had all been part of the plan, Gaz kissed her once more, and the band began their rocking two-hour set. Alicia did periodic checks to make sure that everything was okay, but whenever she could, she stood backstage, closed her eyes for just a moment, listened to Gaz singing, and pretended that he was kissing her again.

Just before the clock struck midnight, Alicia found Sarita and her mom sitting side by side on beach chairs on the wettest part of the sand. They were both barefoot, holding their shoes; as the tide came in, it splashed warm water around their ankles.

"Hi, Sarita and Ms. Lopez," Alicia said. "I hope you're having a good time."

"Oh, my God," Sarita said. "Are you kidding me? This is the best night of my life. I'll never forget it as long as I live. I'm telling you, Alicia, you can read about *quinces*. You can go to a million of them. But you'll never know how magical it is until it happens to you."

Alicia felt a twinge of jealousy that she suspected she'd been fighting back for a long time. Why had she chosen a trip over a *quinceañera*? Looking at all the people dancing and Gaz playing hard-core reggaeton onstage, she felt sad. She'd missed out on all of this, and now there was no going back. The only thing she could do was to make Amigas a huge success, so that more girls like Sarita could get the *quinces* of their dreams.

Alicia reached into her purse, took out an envelope, and handed it to Sarita's mom.

"What's this?" she asked.

"Your change," Alicia said. "I promised you we'd come in on budget, and we managed to come in *under* budget. That's a check for fifteen hundred dollars."

"You keep it," Sarita's mom said.

"No, please, it's the least I could do, considering you took such a big chance on us."

But Ms. Lopez shook her head. "It's an investment. For your business. You've certainly earned it."

Alicia's mind was racing. Fifteen hundred dollars in pure profit. They could rent an office. Buy equipment. Take out advertising. Or maybe she could put it in the bank and start planning their next *quince*, which she had no doubt would be coming up soon. She was all out of business cards, and so were the other members of the group. Though she had the sneaking suspicion that Gaz—in protest against the club's name—had thrown his away.

Walking back to the dance area, she saw Carmen, who came up to her and threw her arm around her best friend's shoulder.

"You did good, *chica*," Carmen said.

"So, you would hire the Amigas?" Alicia said, with a mischievous twinkle in her eyes.

"Of course," Carmen said.

"Excellent," Alicia said. "Because your fifteenth birthday is only a few months away, and I've got *lots* of ideas."

ACKNOWLEDGMENTS

I'm grateful to Jane Startz, Christy Fletcher, and Melissa Chinchillo for inviting me to be part of Amigas Inc. Thank you to Wendy Lefkon and Elizabeth Rudnick for making my words shine as brightly as a *quince*'s tiara. *Besos y abrazos* to Cecilia and Toño Ortega, Diana and Buster Richards, Keith and Digna Downs—you make me proud to be Panamanian and proud to be a Latina. Finally, *mi corazón a Flora y Jason. No hay palabras.*

—*V.C.*

A big thanks to our two wonderful editors, Elizabeth Rudnick and Wendy Lefkon, and to my devoted agent and dear friend, Amy Berkower. With deep gratitude to Veronica Chambers for helping to bring these wonderful characters to life.

—*J.S.*

A Chat With
Jennifer Lopez

When I first came up with the idea for Amigas I thought about the many Latina women who, like Alicia, Jamie, and Carmen, had started out as entrepreneurial teenagers. Who, through hard work, imagination, and dedication, were able to take their passions and talents and become role models and successful adults. For me, Jennifer Lopez is such a woman. She has incredible drive and an amazing work ethic, qualities she shares with the girls in Amigas. They, too, needed an equal amount of determination to turn their quince-party-planning business into a huge success.

So, to get a better sense of this connection, I sat down with Jennifer, and we talked about quinces and what it was like for her to be a Latina girl growing up in New York City....

—J. Startz

1. Did you have a *quince*? If so, what was it like? If not, did you celebrate this right of passage in any other way? As an adult, do you ever regret this decision or wish that you had had one?

I did not have a quince, and looking back, I wish I had! When you are fifteen, you don't always think about what's "special" but more about what's "fun." I had a great party, but now I wish I had celebrated with a full court and everything. Just to think of all the preparations, the dance rehearsals, and the the party itself—it would have been a great memory to have.

2. Do you think more Latina girls today are having *quinces* than when you were fifteen? If so, why do you think this is?

I imagine that it might be less, due to our economy, unfortunately. But I truly think it all depends on the individual family. Hopefully, every Latina girl will get the opportunity to have a quince *or at least the choice to have one. I believe most Latino parents start discussing it when their daughters are young teens.*

3. You're a mom now; when your daughter Emme turns fifteen, are you planning on having her celebrate her quinceañera?

I would love to have one for her. But growing up in the U.S. is so different from growing up in Mexico or Puerto Rico, where my family is from. When you're born in a country where Spanish is the dominant language, it's expected that you have a quince, *but here we're given a choice. I'd like to give my daughter a choice and hope she decides to have a* quince.

4. Which of the *amigas* do you think you are most like and why?

I relate most to Alicia. We are both passionate, creative, fiery, and strong-willed, but underneath it all we're softies!

5. All the members of Amigas Inc. have very strong interests that they want to pursue professionally. When did you know what you wanted to do for a career? How did you get your start?

I always knew that I wanted to perform. I began to book jobs as a dancer, yet I also had dreams of singing and acting. I feel so blessed that I've been able to pursue all my passions and do what I love.

6. You are an internationally successful businesswoman; what advice would you give to young people like the *amigas,* who want to start their own business?

Be prepared to work hard, and go for it! If you stay focused on your goals and maintain a strong work ethic—you can achieve anything.

7. You are an inspiration for millions of Latina girls around the world. What advice can you give them? And what inspired you to become involved with this story?

I love the message that Amigas *give us. Alicia and her friends are wonderful role models for all girls, and I really responded to the idea that even though you are young, you can still begin to fulfill your dreams. These girls are real entrepreneurs!*